What Happened to the Miracle

A NOVEL

by
Meri Robie

Ariadne Press
Rockville, Maryland

Copyright © 2001 by Meri Robie

Library of Congress Cataloging-in-Publication Data

Robie, Meri, 1972-
    What happened to the miracle : a novel / by Meri Robie.
      p. cm.
    ISBN 0-918056-12-8
      1. Women scientists--Fiction. 2. Unmarried mothers--Fiction.
3. Mothers and sons--Fiction. 4. Suburban life--Fiction. I. Title.

PS3568.O263 W47 2001
813'.6--dc21   00-068240

Jacket Design: Leslie Murray Rollins
Typesetting: Barbara Shaw

This book is a work of fiction. Names, characters, places and incidents are either products of the author's imagination or are used fictitiously. Any resemblance to actual events or persons, living or dead, is entirely coincidental.

Publication date:
October 2001
160 pages, $21.95

Ariadne Press
4817 Tallahassee Ave.
Rockville, Maryland
20853

Tara + Dave,

Thank you so much for coming to the reading — it's so very great to know you guys. Please stay in touch with me, as I really love having you around.

love,
Mari R[...]

PART 1

Miracle Birth

1. In the Beginning

The night I decided to move my son, Julian, and myself out of the city was the night I finished a terrible fight. As I watched the city's blank nightwise streets loosely punctuated by the bleeding and cooling lights of police cars, or the bleeding, bandaging lights of ambulances, I saw what seemed to be a broken man's skeleton stretched tightly across the bay. This city had been my opponent for years, the challenge of making it alone, living in desperate conditions, trying to figure out how I could have so easily lost something as precious as my sister. Now I saw a city that was shrinking with the heat of its own bodies. I saw a city where every day people left for a place with more culture, more drive, more art, more money and more self-esteem.

I could not raise my child here. It was an in-between place, a place for stopping and accepting that the rest of your life is upon you. A time for the next choice. Could I find a real terrestrial city, one that might smell like grime and the exhaust of taxis like this place did, but didn't adhere to a bedtime?

I was tired of listening to sirens and to the downstairs neighbors make loud Spanish love. I was tired, too, of the nosy looks I got from the other tenants as I asked my son to help me carry the groceries upstairs. I was tired of waiting for the doorman to return from the bathroom to let me in at night, and I was tired of having my apartment broken into. Three times this year.

I watched my sleeping child, love of my life, barely three years old and already with every single feature the same shape and color and gesture as his asshole father who was not there. Julian had been asleep already by eight that night. There was all this prime time television to watch, so much stuff to think about. And yet, we closed our ears and eyes to it; it might as well not have existed. I barely had the energy to snap on the television. The place was draining me, and I didn't want the city to make Julian hard, get him to distrust my instincts in keeping us in such a spot. The city had given me everything it had. Now it smelled like a corpse.

So did I have to leave for the real country, to find air and stars and sun to sustain us? I didn't want to go home yet, to where my white-trash, cow-patty, bingo-playing, six-rusting-trucks-but-only-one-carport upbringing still hovered in the dark, waiting for me to step back into it, terrifying me with its simplicity and generosity. That left the suburbs for choice. Buy a sensible car, plant begonias, and erect a jungle gym in our yard. Join associations. Die.

But I liked jungle gyms, the plastic seats and the rusty metal. I even liked begonias, though I could barely keep a cactus alive with my black death thumb. I liked the idea of living normally, preserved by the belief that enough is as much as a feast. That no one needs more than an acre to run upon, that mowing grass down to a regulation length and parking your car between two sets of staggered railroad ties expresses the noblest pursuit because of its uniformity, the ease of those rules, and the availability of all supplies to achieve them.

Someone once told me the suburbs happened because the upper middle class designed spaces within the urban centers yet close to the city limits where they could have larger properties. As these edges crowded, the wealthier moved further out and the large chunks of landscaped gardens or servants' quarters that had been part of old estates became cemeteries. People come back in to die. When my sister left me, I went to the city because I believed that that's where the dead went, in towards the center. As you can by the weathered rings of felled trees, you can count how old your city is by the population of the dead. Maybe I'm being melodramatic, since I know that I didn't consider her dead. I still don't consider her dead, but I do consider that if she is anywhere, she must be in the suburbs, her spirit weaving through all the houses, all the bedrooms, all the lives that are happening behind the closed gleaming doors. I've looked into the faces of the city, and even if she were here, she'd be hiding from me, afraid to tell me that she failed. I can't hear her singing voice anymore, but only her shouting. I hear her calling to me with a voice from the dead to come to her, she has left the city on a greyhound bus and she doesn't know where to stop. What can I tell her? But when I get to where I'm going, I think, she'll be welcome there, and we'll have a very long talk.

2. My Son, the Dog

It was a long drive to Folsom and the agent was meeting us at three. Julian held his head out the window; this was his dog phase. This morning he woke me up by barking at the foot of my bed on all fours. Sometimes if I woke late enough, he would already have eaten his breakfast and let some milk dribble a bit down his chin in order to look rabid. The frosty pinks of just budded dogwoods decorated the gravely edges of the Garden State Parkway. During the drive Julian's too-long black hair blew into his face and he pushed it away with a sienna paw. He tried to look into other people's cars. We passed a little Asian boy staring out through the window at Julian. They waved like old friends caught on different lines at the supermarket. He dropped back into the bucket seat and tapped on my right hand.

"Mommy?"
"Yeah?"
"What's a jamboree?"
"It's when people get together and hold a sort of conference."
"What do they do?"
"They celebrate."
"Do they sit in a circle?"
"Sometimes, I guess."
"Can we have a jamboree if we buy a house?"
"Why a jamboree?"
"It sounds like fun. It's a funny word."
"Okay, I don't see why not. As long as the house has a big yard."
"Can we have a dog?"

"You know you're allergic. Besides, I thought you were my sweet puppy."

"Oh, yeah," he smiled and let the wind dry out his tongue. Then he asked, "Can my friends come over?"

"Tell you what: if we buy a house, we'll make sure that all your friends can come over one time and we'll have a giant jamboree. And we'll make hot dogs and eat ice cream and french fries."

"Can we sit in a circle?"

"Sure."

"Can you wear slacks?"

"Slacks?"

"Yes—blue slacks. I think you'd look pretty in blue slacks. And a white shirt. With a flower right here." He drew a little circle on the skin above his heart.

"Sure." I was committing to a jamboree and slacks. I love this kid.

"When are you going to be pregnant again?" he asked.

"I don't know. Why?"

"Miss Jennifer said that Miss Leslie was fat before she had a baby in her. I don't like fat girls."

"I don't want to hear you speak like that. Women come in all shapes and all sizes and they are beautiful, just like men. You can't know if you like someone just because of the way they look. You have to look much much deeper."

Julian was silent for a moment. He started to say something and stopped. Then he said, "Mommy?"

"Yes," still firmly.

"Will I ever have a daddy?"

Up ahead, a flock of about twenty birds swung down in an abortive effort to pick at some roadkill in the middle lane. I moved into the fast lane to let them pick.

"It doesn't look that way."

"Why not?"

"Because I wanted you. I wanted a baby, but I didn't want to marry anybody."

Julian pulled on my hand and licked my fingers. Then he nestled his head into my hip and slept for the rest of the drive, his hot little head sweating against my thigh.

When we arrived, Julian was still very sleepy. He was given to insomnia, now, at age four, and last night he was up all night smacking his blocks together or waging war with his toy soldiers or pretending to read. However, the sleep always catches up with him the next day and he crashed about halfway through the car ride. My vampire child; I ought to buy him a coffin instead of a race car bed. I left him in the station wagon with the window opened to give him a breeze. Dan, our real estate agent, and I talked about what I wanted and what I didn't. He seemed very enthusiastic about the last house on our scheduled itinerary, but wanted to be fair to the other sellers and persuaded me, with a wink, just to look.

We looked at about three houses, all with similar faults. I had Julian's sleeping figure slung across my shoulder as I toured the beige and white and brown rooms. Many of the houses seemed to be sinking and I could see wads of paper, fabric or rubber slyly stuffed under the table feet, keeping the furniture from sliding across the polyurethane floors into a wall.

"What was this development before it was a development?" Having recently seen that movie where the bodies burst out of the suburban soil, I fully expected him to say that it had been a graveyard.

"A cranberry bog," he said cheerily, as if it were a feature.

I raised my eyebrows and he rubbed his hands together. Then he rubbed his perspiring brow.

As I bade farewell to the last set of worriedly smiling owners, Dan put his arm around my shoulders and said, "I know you're going to want the next one. I guarantee." He had the sort of accent that didn't allow long e's to be pronounced without the glance of teeth.

The driveway was smooth white and tan pebbles and the house was set back about four hundred yards off the road. The basement windows were striped with weeds, and the height of the frame gave the impression of a ski lodge. Julian was curled across the vinyl seats and I decided to leave him here for the first trip inside.

"You said you grew up on a farm, right?" Dan asked.

"Yep," I said, knowing what he was getting at. It was secluded, aged and had no hint of poverty. It was as rustic and familiar as the cutest little red barn you ever saw, but when you looked inside, it was full of amenities I couldn't have dreamed of.

"This is it, isn't it?" he asked.

I opened the light screen door, it gave with a satisfying creak, the creak of a house that has been settled in and is used to caring for people. I could see almost every part of the house at once, just looking from the foyer. The kitchen was huge with a long wood chef's counter, in case I wanted to cook for a roomful of boys. Or in case they wanted to cook for me. And the workspace was immaculate; most of the other houses seemed to have nicotine colored wallpaper, pastel molds colonizing old water stains, or a fat puddle of congealed grease suspended from the tile behind the range. It was important to me that I not spend the first three months of my life in my new house clad in yellow rubber mittens scraping off what other people had let cake for years or decades. Either the person who lived here wasn't much of a cook, or was a wonderfully obsessive germ freak.

There was a long living room to the left with a fireplace and blue berber carpeting that ran from the lip of the foyer to the back wall. Unfortunately, it ran up about six inches of the wall in a sort of shrugging gesture, but I accepted that as the one easily remedied flaw. (I could put our couch in front of it.) Except for a ghost door (it had been removed; the cellar was a permanent yawn) to the unfinished basement, that was the end of the downstairs tour.

We looked at the broken cement walls of the basement, cool and damp even in July. There was space for a washer and dryer. My mind shifted to the fishbowl full of quarters I kept in the city, laundry money. How wonderful it would be to leave my son's underwear in the washing machine overnight. Or for days!

As Dan followed me around the inside of the house, he sat when I sat and stood when I stood. He had done his homework on the needs of a single mom, from close but separate bedrooms to open spaces for me to watch my little boy, but not smother him. Even the spacing of the rails on the banister were thick enough to see through but way too thin for Julian to get his head stuck between. Dan enumerated the established carpools in this development and extolled the quality of the school district, adding that his own children went to school here.

"It's tiny. But since it's just the two of you, it's perfect. Great for a mother and a son," he whispered the last bit, as if in church.

He led me up the stairs. There were two long square bedrooms, one light green carpeted and the other dark blue walled. Both had huge closets with long white bars that would put our wardrobes to shame. The wood still smelled very slightly like other people's dust, like the spiciness of overworn socks or the heady sourness of a pile of laundry, though I was uncharacteristically nostalgic for it. It was as if this house were too new, too clean, like a trick. It was like one of those dreams where you see the most perfect house in the world and you go through the door just to realize that it's all a movie set. I didn't trust what I was seeing. The bathroom sat asymmetrically between and in favor of the smaller room. It had a hot tub and held an echo. The sink was the first one in my househunting that someone had bothered to scrub down and it looked shiny and glistening white. Dan took out a pad of paper and a red pen.

"It's what the owners are asking. It's well within your range," he winked as the pen scratched its candy confident flourish across the white of his note pad. Two lines stabbed through the dollar sign almost in a v-shape. I sighed.

A mottled Norway maple branch tapped gently against the broad bay window of the master bedroom which opened out to the roof. We stepped out and I looked over the neighborhood. It wasn't high enough to see much except the roofs of other houses. I heard a mower start up at a house somewhere to my left, but my view of my neighbors' lawns was completely obscured. I did see my bird-dropping spattered car in the driveway. I looked back to Dan and said, "I just want to get a second opinion," and stepped back into the sunny empty bedroom.

I went back to the car to wake up my warm rosy child. His hair was matted to his head and his mouth was open slightly. I watched his rapid breath for just a moment before kissing his ear and whispering to him to wake up. His brown blinking eyes and sleep-settled frown were discarded as quickly as a GI Joe ground strike at the sound of the summer ice cream truck.

He held my hand timidly as we walked inside. His mouth was agape at the wonder of a new house. He rushed up the stairs, his hair and hands flying.

"Mommy!" he bellowed from the closet in what he chose as his room, (fortunately the one opposite the one I'd selected as mine). "Mommy!"

"Yes?"

"I want to put all my friends in here." He caromed off the walls of the closet as he spun.

"Why would you want to keep your friends in a closet?" I smiled and asked.

"Because that's where I'm going to put my toys." He stopped spinning and dropped his arms.

"What about the rest of the room?"

"I want to have an airport here." He blinked up to the ceiling. "Zhooom, zhooom!" He threw his arms out and flew around the room. "And they can land on your bed. Everybody could fly in this house." He ran out to the banister and looked down to the parquet hallway. It was gorgeous. Dan beamed his perky smile, the commission calculating, not coldly, in his eyes. I could picture his family, his wife whispering to him about the kids continuing their piano lessons, three mortgage payments paid in advance. He'll bring her a gift tonight—pumpkin pie, fresh from their favorite nearby bakery. And like wise settlers after a good harvest, they'll feel secure about making it through the winter. In a burst of this good fortune, he called my son, "hey, Tiger."

"I'm a dog!" Julian shouted and dropped to all fours and wiggled his bottom. Dan smiled at me sadly as I petted Julian on the head and scratched his ears.

What Happened to the Miracle

❖

Three months later, though we were still living largely out of boxes, we were pretty much settled in. Julian had made new friends, though we still wrote letters together to the old ones, and I had met a few neighborhood women. I congratulated myself for squeezing the length of our daily route from house to his day care and to my new work down to twenty-three minutes on a sunshiny low-traffic day. I had the house to myself as Julian was sleeping. It was his first real nocturnal sleep since we moved to the new house, and it was hauntingly quiet. I waited in the dark in his room twice just to listen to him breathe, but then I realized I couldn't sleep. I crawled out to the roof to smoke a joint. I hadn't smoked in a really long time, since before Julian at least. I found one joint in a cedar cigar box along with my diploma and my cap and tassel. College was so long ago I supposed the pot would not have any effect, but as I choked down the first hit, I remembered what being high was like and I lay back on the roof to regard the sky.

I grew up on a farm in Barnesville, Ohio. There weren't many kids nearby, and what my parents told us to do if we were bored was to run. I ran for miles out in the fields. I ran the length of the fence, the perimeter of our three hundred acre farm, and back. The smell of the sheared sheep sweating and panting in the barn came back to me, and the smell of my own sweat after running and running. I would run and stop and sweat down, feeling the dry parts of my clothing soak up and feel my long brown hair try to dry while the water continued to pour from my scalp. I loved the feeling of just raining. My brothers and I had games to see who could fit in the little space between the electric fence and the low stone wall that designated the neighbor's property, and we broke off pieces of the salt licks and sucked on them like popsicles.

Anna May, my older sister, left just as Zeke was born. I was eleven years old and I remember how she woke me in near dawn, even though she was hardly ever one to wake before noon unless she had to. Anna May was slender and the only really beautiful woman in our family. She braided my hair and applied lipstick to me for my tenth birthday. She sewed me hippie outfits with embroidery and twisted beaded necklaces around my neck. She loved me even though I was skinny and had a fat nose and was generally ugly. Anna May Eden became simply 'Miracle,' (one name, like Cher) and boarded a bus to Los Angeles in the spring of 1967. That was the last we heard from her. She did not call on the day she was supposed to arrive, nor the day after, nor the next month. George, my older brother, was drafted three months later to Vietnam. My father wouldn't go find her, nor did he let another one of his children on a bus anywhere unless accompanied by my mother or himself. When Zeke and I watched television, I would point out pretty girls and say, "Look! There's Anna May, your sister!"

The first time I changed Julian's diaper, I was wonderfully impressed with the little sticky tabs disposable diapers have on them. Zeke's diapers always had to be emptied and scrubbed out and then boiled in their own laundry pot. Then they were either dried over the stove or lain out in the sun. Zeke would scream if they were the slightest bit wet when we put them on, but Julian was spoiled. He had every plastic toy he ever wanted and the diapers I bought him had ridiculous gimmicks that told you your baby's ass was dry because of the material they were lined with. But then menstrual pads had evolved in time as well. There were always new ways to get things one more level cleaner, it seemed.

I closed my eyes up on this roof. There were sounds of the faraway highway, cars hushing by and sounds of nighttime birds and insects. There was a cool breeze that shivered me only a bit, so my teeth chattered, but my heart was warm. And I remembered drugs like these, how my teeth would chatter no matter how warm I was when I smoked pot. I pulled my windbreaker farther up over my shoulders.

Kansas State had given me a full scholarship but I transferred to the east coast during my junior year. God, how ambitious I was! I am not proud of some of the ways I got my money: I would prowl around the emptied classrooms between periods and find books students might have left under their chairs. I would return the books to the local bookstores for money. Or I would write papers for people under the guise of tutoring them. I was lonely then too. I always seemed to be alone during college. I remember dreaming of social events and parties and I would wake alone, with my books waiting for me to deshelve them and learn, to bother again.

I fell in love with the ideas of people, but I learned not to trust them. Conversations always closed abruptly, as if the other person had been idly tugging on the cord to a set of Venetian blinds and they fell suddenly and completely, signaling the end of the potential of a moment.

This joint was a gift from a girl I knew. I tutored her (wrote two of her papers) and she paid me in marijuana. I liked it. I smoked alone, in my room. I usually slept right after smoking because I would get so hungry and I had no money for food. I developed a sense of knowing where food could be found: I would choose to help one student over another depending upon whether they might have a jar full of candies or a box of saltines nearby or not. A graduate student I knew would put out cookies and I wrote every paper she had assigned for her English class because I was so hungry.

Here I am now, I thought, as I touched the ridged textures of the shingles on my roof. This is a roof that I will have to fix if it breaks, but this is my roof. I have paid for it. I thought these things and felt peaceful knowing that I was self-reliant. In control. How could a girl who used to suck on salt and steal hard candies come to this?

I was not long in Folsom, but I could already feel myself slipping down into anonymity. It was just so easy to buy the prefab house, to have a landscaping company mow and trim, to stand outside a Bennigan's at eight-o'clock on a Friday night, waiting for a muffled approximation of "Eden, party of two" to blurt from a concealed loudspeaker. It was easy to not worry about locking my house, or not to care whether people noticed what was in my shopping cart, or to wear sweat pants until three p.m. on a Saturday, if not all day, and to not go to Sunday mass. It was easier to watch sitcoms and feel that it was true, that what your life was about was being meticulously satirized on prime time TV, or worse, that you could live vicariously through that, have your humorous moments read aloud by thin, pimpleless faces punctuated by the coaxed outbursts of a studio audience that taught you when to laugh. It was horrible, but easy. I felt myself signing up for it all, and I felt the noncommittal shrug that said to me, "you're thirty years old with a child and your life is not tragic. Just take the goddamn Volvo and shut up." I decided I was okay with that.

I remember walking on the beaches of New Jersey for the first time, after I'd moved east and I'd gotten used to the New Jersey accents. It was September and there were scattered sunbathers left over from that terribly hot summer. Tanning was in vogue then, and all the dark honey and burnt toast hues and salty sweet green of the water was overwhelming. Walking was like walking on mud, but harder and my calves were ripe with pain as I walked back to the car. All the license plates I saw were from Pennsylvania (New Jerseyites, I learned, went to LBI). I was slim, then. I wore a bathing suit that has fallen out of style, a lime-green maillot that cut low on the breasts and low on the thighs. But everything is only in my memory; I have never owned a camera.

My son was sleeping. It had taken a long time to get him down tonight, the routine of holding our breath and counting to ten, of counting sheep, of lullabies sung to his wide awake stare, of reading chapters of books so dull they made me drowsy. But those were the times I loved so much. Those were the times I felt most useful, rubbing the small expanse between his small shoulders, believing my body was given special powers with the birth of Julian. I would tell him that there was magic in my hands, sleep magic, that a wizard put into my palms so that I could be a good mother. I told him that there were tea bags of sleep sewn into the tops of his eyelids and if he would close his eyes and look up, he would get tired. Sometimes we spent only ten or fifteen minutes waiting for him to fall asleep, but sometimes it took all night and in the first velvety bluening of the black sky, he might or might not surrender to his exhaustion. Sometimes I would wake up on his bed to him running his hands through my hair or touching my eyelids. It was every night, at least for a while, that he couldn't sleep, but it was the one thing unfailingly that we did together.

I wished my son would cry out to me. I wanted it to be immediate, his need for my arms, my breath, my comfort. I wanted him to hold me as if he was falling off the edge of the world and I was the only thing he could rely on, hold on to, believe in. I wanted him to wake *right now* and come tell me that he loved me, to pull on my hair and push his head into my belly screaming for what he understood as life before he wriggled his way out, screaming for the place where thought was soupy but pure, things known were really known because existence was not questioned. Right then his eyes were seeing that life, vibrating madly across the backs of his eyelids, viewing the cavalcade of personifications, perceptions and hopes, dreams, hurts, passions and glut that he swept through gently that day. It wouldn't make sense when he woke up, but it is important that it couldn't. His dreams of witches stirring scary bubbling brews and strange men with crooked noses introducing themselves and offering baseball tickets would terrify his little conscious brain, and it's the safety of his sleeping body that protected him. He dreamed of cats lying half flattened in the road, shrieking in pain, and pickles floating in jars, and the way waking replaces all the fears with the tangible, the feeling of his spoon in his hand as he dug into his cereal, the sound of the fire truck somewhere in the distance, the benevolent smiles of muppets and basketball stars on the posters in his room. My son's world was alive, filling up the house with images and I was outside, letting my house fill, letting it all overflow believing that when I went to sleep, I would have his beautiful colors and shapes and faces and needs to warm me, to pull me by the hand calling, "Mommy, Mommy! Look, I'm sleeping!"

❖

 Closer to the highway, the neighborhood sprawl shrank to simple lunchbox-shaped houses and moth-eaten lawns secured by four-foot green chainlink fences. Julian was visiting a new friend on the other side of our development and I walked to pick him up. It was the longest day of the year and full of the kind of sun that impregnates the air with the artificially fresh smells of the bed sheets pinned to clotheslines that look like TV antennae. One of the tiny houses was closing down a yard sale. There were large blankets splayed upon the lawn proffering linens in every shade of mauve, and stiff green and pink children's clothing draped across three concrete steps up to the front door. I have always been repulsed by yard sales. The idea of someone else's sicknesses and sloppiness residual in the fabric disgusts me. Even when I was little I would be very careful to wash inherited clothing that I would only wear if it was from Anna or my mother.
 A hardened little woman conducted business with a cigarette clenched in her teeth. When she spoke, the butt rolled around on her tongue like she was rearranging a toothpick. She squinted from beneath her pea green visor and stuffed bills into and extracted change from her fanny pack. I was loathe to stop but I was intrigued by a kid who must have been her son. He was about fifteen and one of his legs was slung into a thigh cast. His pappy arms struggled with a chipped pine night table and I could see it slipping from his thin, birdlike fingers. I was caught watching the object slip, watching him about to receive a smack or a screech from the harpy on the lawn. There were about six feet between me and the kid and as much as I wanted this to be his victory, I knew it wouldn't be, and I lurched in to help. He slipped and I overestimated the weight of the thing and almost lost my balance. The kid's brown eyes looked up at me and I saw this thankful puppydog expression and I was glad to help, to be here to save him this one potential grievous reprimand and to reverse, just for an instant, the negative reinforcement that I remember hating when I was a kid growing up a klutz, growing up ugly and alone and poor.

What Happened to the Miracle

❖

My father was never a particularly nice man. Most of my looks are from him, including my fat nose. He wasn't so much ugly in the unattractive sense of the word as an ugly person. He laughed at us when we failed and he called me a show-off for reading so early. For about a month, because I was sick of him coming down on me for reading all the time, I read with a flashlight in to my bed late at night, while listening to Anna talk and toss about in her sleep. Even now I need some sort of noise when I read or else my mind starts wandering.

He would tell us a story about his brother, Gary, when they grew up on the farm. His brother died in a tractor accident way before I was born. My father had pictures of them together, arms slung across each other, my father a stout, knobby nosed, pitted-faced man with small eyes and his brother, a broad-chested, happy but daft type who still donned overalls even though he was well over thirty. Apparently my father and his brother were horsing around as teenagers trying to impress the Hoople girl, Sally. Sally's brother Dave dared my father to play matador with their cantankerous old fat bull, Warlock. My father was two years younger than Gary, so Gary stepped in as the hero. Looking to impress Sally, he whipped off his red satin baseball player's jacket and shook it in front of the bull. The bull paid no attention, so Gary ran towards him and jumped up and down, kicking up dust and screaming at the sedentary bull. When Gary made him mad enough, Warlock began to charge, but Gary was the fastest runner on the baseball team and got a good lead. He spun around, stepped out of the way and grabbed one of the bull's horns, yanking its neck to the side and flipping the huge black stinking bull upside down. My father swore that the force of the bull landing on the earth was enough to shake both Sally and Dave from their perches on the wooden fence between the properties. The bull eventually had to be put down for back problems a year after that, but none of the kids, Dave, Sally, Gary nor my father, ever said anything about the incident except to brag about it to us, long after the elder Hooples were dead. We were bound by a sacred pact with our father. We sat around the fire and heard this story over and over and over. It was the only story he shared with us and we only sat because we had to. He was very quick to beat us and short of praise.

But he was right about one thing: I was so clumsy. It seemed everything I touched was broken as or soon after I touched it. Once, as I was playing with one of my mother's Christmas ornaments, a Waterford crystal octahedrite that my parents had received from one of my grandmother's debutante friends, in my clumsy fingers it suddenly became a heptahedrite, and a simple icicle shard like a sterilized murder weapon sat in my palm. As a child, I never lied, but even if I had, I was too late to make reparations. My mother, sensing disaster due to my proximity to the Christmas tree, crept across the unfinished wood in her bare feet and slapped me on the back of my head. That sent both the steeple of glass and the sacred ball it had been a part of out of my hands and into the wall behind me where it broke into no fewer than twenty pieces. We stared at it, horrified. I wanted to cry. My mother asked me, "Why do you always do this to me? Do you hate my things? Should we just not have nice things in this house?" I thought she was being serious. When I think back to it, she still sounds serious, as if I were a black cloud that rained hammers onto her precious crystalline life. I felt like I was hurting her. She let me read from then on, and discouraged my father's jokes about my four eyes and whirligig hat brain and all the other mean things he said to me.

My father changed when Anna left, though. He left himself. They were never on very good terms with one another, but there must have been a bond - something keeping them together, an understanding maybe, because he lost it when she left. Not only did he stop paying attention to the amount I studied or read, but he stopped paying attention to us all altogether. It could have been that Zeke was born, and he was a lost, frightening child who acted more like a bull than a boy. His eyeballs would roll around the bloodshot whites of his eyes and he would charge at you, bursting into your personal space, but he would never touch you. He grunted and said few understandable words, even into his teens. Maybe it was the leaving of Anna and the coming of Zeke, like a lion and a lamb (or a lion and a bull), but he became strange. He started organizing everything in our house, for one thing. All the cleaning products were arranged in alphabetical order of their jobs. Because none of us could keep track of how they were supposed to sit on the shelves, he made labels. Then he started cleaning all the sponges in the house with hot bleach. He would wander off and we would find him sitting on a fence watching the Hoople's old bull, Thor, wander around his pen, dropping fat black wretched smelling patties and eyeing my father threateningly. My father got confused sometimes and he would smack the kitchen table to make an announcement that would have one or two nonsense words tucked into it. George and I didn't really fear him, but we nervously laughed, as if it were a joke we were all in on. Whatever you did to my father, you never laughed at him. I watched Anna get whipped for that.

My mother, however, began to say things under her breath. All her life with us, she was straightforward, never afraid to speak her mind. These things started slipping out under her breath and it was like an evil presence in the house, like a demoness couched in those words. She would say, "It would be good to have a real man around this place," and then she would kick my father's feet as we sat on the porch. As if this weren't bad enough, she would add, "useless," or "loon," so softly you could barely hear her. She took liberties saying things she might have thought would have driven him crazy, like she was testing the waters. "If I die tomorrow," she'd say. Then to us, "I'm not so young anymore."

They lived like that for years, until I called from college and learned that my father had had his first stroke. After that, for him, it was just a matter of time. The strange thing is that shortly after that first stroke, I came home to music.

My father was always insistent that good music ended with Benny Goodman. He hated rock and roll, be-bop, Motown (which he referred to with less pretty names) and anything less than big band. Anna once voiced that she wanted to be a music critic and he threw a shoe at her shouting that no one who can listen to the Grateful Dead without puking should be able to judge music. As far as I remember, she threw the shoe back but didn't have a ready retort. At any rate, if we were to play music, it had to be big band.

When I came home that weekend, the windows of the place were opened up and I heard a beautiful voice singing the jazz standard "Ain't Misbehaving." It was such a soulful, exuberant voice I thought, Ella? Dinah Washington? Who?

It was my mother. She was dancing around the kitchen frying potatoes, adding spices, singing *a cappella.*

"Mom! That's beautiful," I complimented.

She kept humming and swung me around the kitchen. We danced like an old couple, her breath near my ear carrying a lovely sweet perfect thread of music, tempered now that her audience was so close. As she finished up she held me at an arm's length. Her hair was half flopped out of its usually severe bun and though she was usually barefoot around the house, today like no other day she moved on her toes. She looked radiant and joyful; I was stunned.

"I used to sing in high school," she said. "Cut these carrots into strips." She handed me a colander of peeled carrots, their orange flesh glowing with the sunlight that poured through the windows. She kept on singing and I chopped and wondered what kind of monster my father was and if this is what my mother would be like if she'd always been free.

3. Jamboree

I wore slacks. I wore blue slacks with white brocade stripes, as ugly as you can imagine that to be. I borrowed a pants suit from my mother and Julian was ecstatic. Some of the other mothers I had met through community meetings helped put some stands together. Apparently, Julian had heard of a jamboree from one of his playmates in school whose brother was a boy scout. We had several boy scouts there, in uniform, holding their mothers' hands and looking bewildered. We had a rope pull and a basketball hoop that we tied to a chestnut tree in the backyard. Girls and boys both were invited. Julian and I left the backyard ruined by discarded paper cups and plates still containing food and chewing gum stuck to the grass. We watched it out the window, daring the non-biodegradables to biodegrade. Finally I felt the motherly cord in my back snap and I said "that's it." We tied tee-shirts over our mouths and wore big gloves and every time he shrank from something (or I shrank from something) I said aloud, "It will wash off." We filled only two double-ply Heftys and rewarded ourselves with a quick shower and full bowls of ice cream.

During the jamboree, I met some of the neighborhood women. They invited me to join their Junior Women's Club, which met at the YWCA on Thursdays. Molly, a dynamo who enjoyed donning clown suits whenever she got the chance, was the leader. This, I only gleaned from the other ladies who interpreted her mock sign language; she couldn't speak today since real clowns don't talk. Her big teeth, yellowish in contrast to the white clown face makeup, glowed at me while she mimed lifting a phone off its receiver and, having dialed the pretend numbers, held the imaginary receiver to her ear.

Marta and Anise were sisters-in-law. They were big, happy red women who seemed to always know what their children were doing. I let Julian chew on a dandelion for a minute and their eyebrows rose in tandem to absurd heights. Quickly I reprimanded my son and brushed the yellow petals from his tongue with my fingers. When I looked back to the table, Anise was holding out a pre-moistened towelette package to me, thermally heated by her palms and the paper torn just a bit at the top, the way I give Julian his bags of potato chips. After that I just followed their leads. When Anise's Sally was pushing her little brother off the swing set, I lifted my eyebrows and she called out "Sally!" The little girl opened her palms in front of her and shrugged while her little brother stuck out his pink tongue. I was getting the hang of the signals and beginning to feel more like a mothering force—the Mom Team. Grrr.

Jane was the overprotective mother. I think every team whose members are comprised of mothers has one desperately overprotective one. Every word she said she gently patted and smoothed into the gingham tablecloth for emphasis and she had a telling little wobble that hid behind each word she uttered as if she was always just barely containing rage. She may very well have slipped these idiosyncrasies into the gene cocktail that grew into her son, Emanuel, since, as he tried to explain his position on sandbox sharing and the sort of playing partner he'd rather have, he also patted his words into the table, pressed them down and made them stick, as if logic were a kind of glue. He, however, was not as adept at controlling his anger. When his carefully unfolded reasoning failed to persuade the panel of mothers, he tossed himself onto the ground and kicked and pulled at the dirt and newly seeded bluegrass (not that I cared; I had lawn boys). Jane just turned to us with an uncomfortable smile, the smile of a woman who is considering much too much pertinent advice at once. When he was finally exhausted he just lay on the ground, his face wet with tears staring blankly at our Keds and fat calves. One tier above, we all exchanged knowing glances. Julian wandered over to me at this point and brushed back my hair to ask into the cup he made around my ear, "What happened?"

"Manny is upset because his mother won't let him play with the big kids."

He seemed to consider this for a moment.

"Can I ask him to play with me?" he whispered.

"Sure, sweetie." I watched as Julian carefully approached him and lay down beside him. Manny turned his face over towards Julian and they talked for a minute. Suddenly, they both scrambled up and away.

Jane asked me, "What do you do? He's so generous!"

I had to admit that there were many times he really let me down: the recent tantrum he threw concerning alleged chemicals in the cellophane-wrapped chicken at the supermarket and the (less recent) time I thought that he wasn't going to stop screaming in Macy's unless I hit him. I painfully recalled the time his head was lodged between the curiously narrow bars of the banister in my mother's house and we actually had to saw him out. And there was the night after night of staying up with my sick child, his allergies to breast milk causing a blooming cranberry sauce colored rash in his diaper and knitting a self-esteem complex in my heart.

But it's not true that I was embarrassed of him. I see these moms with leashes on their kids, or I see these kids who are way too big for strollers slung into them like sacks of dog food in the supermarket or the mall, the rubber tips of their sneakers idly snagging the linoleum and their mothers comparison shopping or making appointments with babysitters or bosses on cell phones. These are the women who hit their kids when they do anything, have any expressions at all. These are the moms who instill in their kids the notion that the most important asset in life is learning to sit still. These are the moms who see their children as natural extensions of themselves and they don't *like* themselves, so they take it out on their kids. I'm not like these people. I love it when my kid does something that I didn't expect.

There are certainly a lot of sacrifices he's had to make in his life. He couldn't know his father because of me and so he got me, full force, one hundred percent maternal. He's had to spend a lot of time in day care, and he's not allowed to watch TV. I've often thought about how much I need him and whether it's okay for a kid to feel needed by a grown-up. Maybe it is intimacy, the way we are just ourselves all the time. Maybe we're just good people and because there are no pretenses, we just get along.

"I don't know," I said. "I guess I don't have anyone to contradict me when I want to do something my way."

Molly's lips spread a compassionate clown smile across her face. Jane still looked worn out from the last episode, and Anise and Marta nodded and said, "Isn't that the truth?"

Anise said, "You know, I've offered to all the other ladies here the use of our inground pool. Anytime you and Julian feel like taking a swim, please do."

Molly mimicked the breaststroke and made fish faces. Jane started to laugh and Molly pulled a deflated blue balloon out of her breast pocket and bloated it lengthwise in one graceful exhalation. I was glad to see it was not for us, but for several children who gathered around her to watch.

It always felt natural to accept love from Anna May when I was growing up. George made fun of us, walking hand in hand into town. He called us lesbians and incest-sisters, a term that he shaved down to 'Incesisters' by the time I was six. It was, perhaps, the cleverest thing he ever said; he wasn't the most intelligent of boys. I used to crawl into Anna's bed often—I never wanted to be without her body by my side.

She started running away just after I was born, but she never attempted to abandon me. My mother told me a story about Anna running once. She said that she left my father to watch me when she discovered that Anna was gone. She found Anna May about two miles from our house, swinging a cardboard suitcase. My mother drove up to her in the truck and ordered her to get in. Although Anna complied, she wouldn't put the suitcase on the flatbed, but held it in her lap, tapping it and hugging it occasionally. As my mother drove the truck back onto our property, my father came running to the cab of the truck. He tore the passenger side door handle off, and pulled Anna out of the car by her hair. The suitcase must have tumbled to the ground at this point. My father screamed at Anna May, "What did you do to the baby?" meaning me. Anna knelt in the dirt and unsnapped the lid of the suitcase to reveal me, smiling and gurgling, very carefully tucked into clothes that had the softest fabrics, a couple slices of bread, a bottle of sugared water, and two cloth diapers. My mother told it as a very sweet story—one of the days when Anna May's heart really was in the right place. Of course, it terrified me to know that somehow I had been trapped in a suitcase for a couple hours and had fallen inside that suitcase onto the hard ground from a height of at least four feet. My mother reached over to me and told me that I wasn't hurt in the slightest, saying, "maybe if I'd dropped all of you from four feet up, you'd all be chemists instead of spread all over the world."

Whenever I talked to Anise and Marta and Molly and Jane, I tried to picture them as little girls. It was obvious that Molly was probably the girl who consistently scored the lead in the school play. Other girls were jealous of her, but too lazy to do anything about it. Marta and Anise were the types of women whom I couldn't imagine were not mothers at one point. Marta showed me pictures of her with her husband once, in the mid-seventies, fishing naked near a log cabin. She said, "don't think I wasn't getting bitten by mosquitoes, 'cause I was." I didn't think I would be so much younger than she was, but then she told me that the picture was taken when she was sixteen. I couldn't imagine anyone sixteen and blissfully uncovered in my house. Ours was a strict religious house complete with crucifixes over each of the beds and the illustrated Bible to read at night. My father wasn't particularly religious, but he was God-fearing. The thing that infuriated him the most of all the things Anna May ever did was when she was fifteen, on a brisk October day, she went out into the yard and stripped off all of her clothes.

"I don't want nothing of yours!" she yelled at the house. My mother came out with oven mitts on her hands. My father stepped out of the barn to shake his fist at her, but froze when he saw her standing there naked. "I hate you!" she continued. "I don't want any of your trash!"

I don't know what was the disagreement, but if I ever wondered what it would be like to be naked with my parents around, I found out then. My father threw a horse blanket over her, and that's a rough cloth which probably created some of the scratches she had on her back. But then he smacked her with one of the horse brushes yelling out, "You little hippie slut! I'll teach you to be a hippie slut!"

She kept quiet under that cloth, perhaps crying, perhaps too cold not to be shivering. My mother took her back into the house after my father finished up with her and my mother pulled a softer blanket around Anna May's shoulders.

They shared coffee at the dinner table. Crocheted pumpkin-shaped placemats, jack-o'lantern faces made by curves of embroidered cross stitches, a project shared by Anna and my mother when Anna had just learned to knit, decorated the dusty blue tablecloth. I was sent up to my room while my mother talked with Anna May. I stared out the window watching my father smoke cigarettes near the barn, wringing the arthritic hand he'd used to clench the brush. Finally, my mother stepped outside to gather the clothes that had been discarded in the yard. When Anna May came back upstairs, the smell of maple pecan bread swept in behind her. She dropped the blanket and stood naked in front of me. She had hair in places that I didn't yet and I looked away.

"Look at me, Karen."

"No," I remember I said, quite softly.

"Karen, I've got a woman's body now and someday you will too. It's a beautiful thing. Don't think that a body is ugly and should always be covered up with clothes."

I was all mixed up. I thought my sister's body was the most beautiful thing I'd ever seen in my life and I couldn't look back. It had to be a sin, this looking at your sister's femininity. Something. Even though I was seeing the gingham pattern of my bedspread, I saw the wide bell of her hips, the pig colored flesh of her nipples, the prominent blue vein that trailed down the side of her left breast. I looked back to her, but she had covered herself back up and was no longer looking at me, but at her own reflection in her vanity mirror.

"I'm a virgin, you know," she said as she pulled on a pair of blue jeans. I might have nodded but I didn't understand anything. I waited until she left the room and then resumed my perch watching over the front yard. My father came into the house and I heard the water pipes run as he must have been washing his hands. The edges of the window began to lace with condensation and my mother's voice rang through the floorboards calling me to dinner. I was tired and waited until she came to get me herself.

The next day, Anna May took her savings and bought most of her wardrobe from thrift stores with that money. Once, when she ran out of clothes, she wore a valence curtain as a skirt. She started a fashion trend in school with that curtain, believe it or not, that lasted for about two years localized to ours and the five surrounding towns. She was charismatic, popular and charmed. All of her original clothes were passed down to me and they slumped off my shoulders and dragged on the ground as shapeless bolts of fabric. It took me a long time to approximate her size, but then I grew right past her height out of her clothes.

I can't say that I was a popular child. I was prodigal. That is to say, I was a prodigy—not like the son in the tale. Little, promising signs popped out of my three-four-five-six-seven year old mouth. I was counting at three, reading at four, adding at five, reading full length Victorian novels at six and textbooks at seven. I read everything I could find except my brother's chemistry books. I don't know what repelled me about them, but I abhorred them. I remember reciting lines of poetry to Anna May, quoted from her own textbooks. I remember that her face always displayed such a beguiled, pleased look, but a look wholly devoid of recognition. I read every single poem in her poetry book, looking for one that I could begin, and her voice would sing up and meet mine and we would complete the poem in tandem, making music out of our similar voices, an ethereal match that belied my homeliness contrasted to her beauty. Never once did she join in. However, I found that she would know all the lyrics to Bob Dylan songs, though. And Donovan songs, and Dusty Springfield. Even Leonard Cohen lyrics and the occasional

What Happened to the Miracle

Beatles song would move her, so I abandoned her books and learned her music. She left me the lyrics to *Everybody Knows* written in her lopsided loopy schoolgirl's cursive upon the back of her last incomplete algebra homework as a clue to her vector, the places she was headed to in life, but it was of no use. It could have been any song, but I was left alone all the same. I searched every lyric for a trace. I gave them all up by the time I was thirteen.

I read stories about lost people, people trying to find their way home. I wrote in my diary that it was for her my face was kept in a smile. My face in a jar by the door. I stopped reading textbooks voraciously and scoured the current events in the newspaper. It was the sixties and I was nine-ten-eleven-twelve-thirteen. I read about protests and demonstrations. George told me he would see me in a couple years as he left for Vietnam. He knew that I needed him to come back, he knew how much I distrusted people leaving me since Anna May left. And he did come back, but he, like many GIs, came back changed, disgraced, dishonored. At dinner one night, he stood and reached across the table to slap me for wearing a tee shirt with a flower power slogan on it. I forget what the message was because I tossed the tee shirt into the fireplace after dinner. My mother sent him upstairs after me to apologize, but all he said was, "Anna May wasn't who you think she was. I fought. I should be your hero." I don't think I responded, crying into my pillow, missing her and missing the boy he was and hating my life.

I forgot a lot of things in that mess. I forgot why I was studying so hard, I forgot why I cared about physics and philosophy and literature. I forgot how all the myths went, who married or killed whom, what was Greek, what was Latin and why it mattered. Definitions of words left me as casually as fair weather friends, discreetly checking their watches and slipping out the door, sensing crisis. The delicate calculus proofs that had seemed like such a lovely, fragile language to me now became impenetrable. I had no idea how to graph even simple equations. Physics fell away from me, and I no longer cared how wall switches turned on light bulbs nor how an icebox kept its temperature. Philosophy meant nothing. It became difficult to follow the logic puzzles I had enjoyed so much as a child.

History seemed full of lies and I ached for the truth, for the whole story. The problem was, no one knew it. No one could tell me the answers I was looking for.

I didn't care how energy worked if no one could tell me exactly what energy was, how energy was different than matter. I didn't care what math was if no one could tell me why, if you did out the equation, following all the sums and divisions and exponents, sometimes one plus one equaled three. I didn't care about words that had to be looked up. I denounced such things, just as the other girls and boys in my class did. I denounced them because they didn't get to the point, they didn't give it to me straight. They couched their sinister messages in coddling connotations. They lied.

The only thing then that piqued my interest was chemistry. I read about Watson and Crick, and I wanted solve the genetic puzzle, to know the code. I studied and studied, trying to find why I had blue eyes, where the differences were between me and Anna May, what made our bodies different, what took her away so quickly. I'm still looking, I guess. My major was molecular biology and I completed my masters at Johns Hopkins. When I got out, I went fast and furiously into the Human Genome Project and I remain there today, having contributed several sequences to the project already, and patented two mutated strains of frog DNA in the process.

I totally lost interest in everything but chemistry by the time I was thirteen. It was a terrible two years that I spent in the decline before I found my talent. I also learned to use the minimum of effort to get perfect grades without caring about the subjects. I would absorb the material up to the tests and forget it all immediately afterwards. I kept what I needed to succeed.

It is no coincidence that Anna May left at the beginning of the decline. Or maybe it is sheerly coincidence. Eleven is apparently a critical age for little girls. It was a critical age for me, in 1967, when the world was on fire and rebellion, suspicion and the threat of nuclear annihilation was everywhere. I wore the clothes passed down to me from Anna May's wardrobe. I wore her headbands and I wore her Indian print shirts. I wore her bell-bottoms and her long peasant skirts. I wore her grown up clothes because I had to, because they were all I had. But I never quite fit in them. I looked like the peasant, the outcast. I was the girl, in a world full of love, that nobody loved.

Maybe it was a loss of her presence that hit me so hard. Maybe her beauty, or her faith in me, carried me. No one in school ever really took me as a prodigy—at best I was disciplined, forced to repeat lessons that I had already taught myself, as punishment for subverting the school system. I stopped studying altogether for a time and watched soap operas and listened to rock music. I read newspapers, looking in the obituaries for Anna May's face, her description. I begged my father to let me go to Woodstock, or to march on Washington, or to go to San Francisco, hoping I would see her there.

I would hear water moving in the bathroom in the order she would use it. When she lived with us, she would shower for about ten minutes, pee, and flush the toilet. Then there would be about two minutes of silence while she soaped up her face and let it cake, and then several splashes of water to rinse and cool her skin. I bit my nails aching to burst in sometimes, when I didn't know who was in there. But inevitably the cycle would break part way - no flush following the shower, just the creak of the wooden door as the anonymous bather ignorantly escaped my wrath, or the shower clipped short, signifying an individual with less hair, a gesture of personality that in my tension I found no more mollifying as it became clear that it wasn't her.

I sometimes can imagine a world without privacy and rules, just so if Anna May dropped into a rehab clinic to trade in some dirty needles, or if she stepped on a rusty cola can in her garage and needed a tetanus shot, I could find her. It may be what drove me into genetics, that kind of code, something that would give me a clue as to her whereabouts. Wherever her blood or skin or hair is, maybe that's how I'll know. I've gone over a million different things that I'd say to her now, but I'd probably just cry, just like all those reunited families on talk shows do. I'd probably have too many unusable words stopping up my throat while she just smiled at me and said, "Heya, kid. How's it going?"

I read *Flowers for Algernon* right before she left. When I saw the

Cliff Robertson version of *Charly*, I couldn't stand watching Claire Bloom play Alice Kinian. She was beautiful and remarkable in the role, but I had always pictured Anna May's benevolent, luminescent face. I had pictured Anna May as she struggled against her feelings, knowing that it was the wrong decision to lead him on, and I pictured Anna May as he hurt her. I pictured Anna May, tragic and faithful as she watched his demise. I saw the movie not too long ago with Julian and Alice's part is easily filled by Claire Bloom now. I felt ridiculous for my younger self, who had howled to everyone about how a famous actress had stolen the role her sister was born to play.

And then I stopped wearing her clothes. I hated the smells of them, some like mothballs, some like rain, some like patchouli, some like marijuana, some like horse stables, some like shit. My mother and I laundered them all and packed them away in a large box that we stored in the basement, officially closing the door of hope for her return. Anna May's face never appeared on any movies, television shows, commercials, magazine ads nor even milk cartons. She was eaten up whole, as my mother says.

When the YWCA closed for a week, the meeting of the Folsom Junior Women was held in the local high school little theater, upon the house lighted stage. We sat on folding chairs and drank warm cans of diet soda and ate handfuls of lowfat potato chips. Molly, no longer in costume, led the meeting, accepting suggestions and volunteers for bake sales, yard sales, fund-raisers and dues. I listened to rumors about teachers in the grade school and discussed carpools and part-time jobs licking envelopes.

Our kids played in the audience chairs, sometimes pretending to be our audience, and yawning considerably to let us know they were bored, but more often watching each other perform in the two foot wide expanse between the front row seats and the lip of the stage. Julian did vaudevillian routines he'd picked up from old Fred Astaire movies and the other kids acted out cartoon characters: "*you* be Velma; *I'm* Daphne!" They clapped politely for each other and kept pretty much out of our hair. However, today I could tell they were more restless than usual.

"What's up, guys?" I asked to the wide-eyed bunch of children.

"Julian is telling us lies," answered Anise's child, Sally.

"What is he telling you?"

"That he doesn't have a father."

"That's true."

"But all babies have fathers. Sometimes the father doesn't live with them, but all babies have them somewhere."

This diatribe set off Julian. "Why can't I see my father? Don't I have a father?"

"No, no father. Sometimes if the mother wants a baby enough, she can have a baby all by herself," I lied to the group, and I hoped the mothers would back me up. They didn't.

"What she means to say," began Marta, "is that sometimes the father doesn't want to live with the mother because they have differences."

I'm pretty sure Marta saw my face. She sipped from her plastic cup of soda and then swirled the brown liquid around as if it were fine red wine. She licked a small bit of tan carbonated scum off her lip.

"Julian never had a daddy. Just like baby Jesus never had a daddy. It's that simple."

Anise burst out laughing. Marta looked horrified. Molly's little girl started doing a dance around Julian, singing, "Julian is Jesus, Julian is Jesus." I waited for the whole scene to die down, for the mothers to corral their children and for the mothers themselves to stop being so horrified or laughing, before I spoke again.

Jane leaned over and slapped my leg. "You call yourself a Christian! Shame on you!"

I stood. Julian looked so forlorn and bewildered. "You want to see your daddy? Let's go see your daddy." I stepped down the stairs of the stage and marched out of the room, the Little Theater doors banging shut behind us, and pressed the long red bar on the front door that led out of the school. I'd forgotten that you need a key or you set off the security system. We stepped through the screaming doors, the brick building helplessly consumed in a firestorm of bleating noise. When I looked back, I saw the children gathering like inmates, their faces pressed against the long glass of the school, barely lit by the fluorescent hallway lights tempered by the thick fabric of the curtains. They looked hollow and scared, as if they'd just seen a ghost, met their maker, or they had just become aware that mothers' soothing voices did not always carry information that was true.

I took Julian home and I showed him everything I knew about his father. I showed him the note that his wife left me, and I read it to him, abbreviating the curse words to the word 'expletive' in the diatribe. I showed him the company telephone directory from 1982 that listed his name and his title, Dir. Molec. Bio. DNA Seq. Div. PhD. I explained everything I could to him. When I was done, he said, "I'm not like baby Jesus? I'm not God's baby?"

"Of course you're God's baby," I said. "He gave you to me, right?"

"No. That man did." He pointed to a different name in the book - someone I did not know.

"Were you happier before you were thinking about who your father was?"

He shrugged.

"Sometimes mysteries are more interesting than the truth. Sometimes it's fun just to believe that you are someone you're not, or to make up who you want to be. You can tell me who you want your father to be and we can pretend that's true."

He considered this. Then he said, "No. My father will always be an expletive who didn't want me and you lied to me and never told me."

He ran upstairs to his room and shut the door. It didn't matter that he was over it by the time he woke up in the morning. This was the first time I had to reevaluate the way I saw the world, the things I chose to believe and chose not to. This was the first time I saw myself as a liar. I wondered how I had learned such self-delusion. By two o'clock in the morning, I was still worried that my son, the only person I was sure I loved, still loved me and wasn't ruined by what I had told him all his life. I went into his bedroom and ran my fingers through his hair. I promised him in the quiet blue night, moon as witness, that I would never lie to him again. It would be all harsh truth. And I would have to face things that I had never considered. My first real lesson (other than to ALWAYS accept the epidural when it's offered) of mothering was thus learned. I fell asleep with his small body pressed against me and when I woke up, blinking from the light, and saw him pushing a toy truck around the floor while making "shuuuhrrr" sounds, I hoped I hadn't done permanent damage.

❖

I was in love with Julian's father, for a very brief span of time. I believed I loved him because of what I felt, which is I guess why it's so easy to get pregnant in the first place. I heard him say things to me like, "you really *know* me" and I would see the word "know" curl like vines around the necks of all our shared experiences, those little times when he smiled because I said something he knew was true and good, or those minutes when after kissing, his face and mine would be an inch apart, our features blurred by our proximity, the world in half-light, perfection that seemed attained, and the gathered bouquet he delivered to me like a pure white fistful of daisies.

His intelligence was incontrovertible. He was not only the head of the molecular sciences division at thirty-one years old, who completed his dissertation at twenty-one, but he would write long sexy notes to me with allusions and poetic references. Once after sex, he sat up in bed and wrote a proof of a new way to estimate *pi*. He was an intellectual lover, exploring, charting, evaluating, appreciating me. He kissed parts of my body that I feel icky just touching when I wash. He felt real to me, the most real thing that I had ever done. He never asked me to do anything weird or kinky. It was a beautiful time, two weeks. Yes, I know how short that sounds.

Julian's pet frog died in the clothes dryer. Heard a thump, thump coming from the dryer when I was down there and I thought that it might be something that he left in his jeans pockets, so I didn't investigate. When I pulled out the frog he was stiff and very dry. I tapped him on the white metal edge of the dryer and he sounded like cardboard. I put him in a discarded shoe box and brought him upstairs with the laundry. However, I forgot the shoe box on Julian's bed while I delivered the rest of the laundry to my room. Julian came in with the open box, his face covered in wet tears and mucus. He told me he hated me, left me with the dead frog box and slammed himself into his room. I wanted to let him sulk it off, but I heard him screaming at me from behind his door. He told me that I was old and mean and that I had wrinkles. He told me that it was my fault that he didn't have a father and he told me that I never do anything right. I'm sure I screamed back at him some pretty awful things, but I felt so terrible that I went downstairs and cried. Before I knew what I had done, I was holding part of the telephone in my hand and listening to Abraham's voice on the phone, a recording that was saying "we're not home right now…" I needed someone, anyone, to stop it all so that I could breathe. I had a son I felt like I never saw because I was always at work, staring into tiny microscopes, writing down tiny numbers, an infinity of precision. I wanted to throw it all on the ground, start again, stop being a single mother in a suburban neighborhood paying bills and buying groceries and washing laundry and cleaning toilets and doing all those little repetitive things that you can hand off to your partner these days if you really need to, if you have one. I was feeling so sorry for myself that I guess I asked myself 'who is it that knows what I should do?'

It must have been the time Abraham had come to my apartment in Trenton and in a glorious, delicious gesture swept off all the dishes and glasses on my kitchen table, whipped off the table cloth and made love to me for three hours one night on the table, counter and floor, filling me again and again, making me wetter and happier and more fluid, that I recalled and said, this is a man who will understand right now what I need.

"Beep," said the answering machine. And then silence.

I put down the phone and cleaned off my face in the downstairs sink. I cried. I lay down. I sat up. I cried more. When I was done, I went and knocked on Julian's door. He opened it and threw himself around my waist.

"It's okay," I whispered.

"I never want to make you cry like that again," he said, unaware that the healthiest thing he ever did to me was to be born.

❖

Anise called the next day to tell me that Marta was sorry. We all met for dinner at Molly's house that Saturday, (Molly's affection for wearing that clown suit was almost pathological) and we all made amends. However, this was not the only time I didn't fit in with the Junior Women.

When Julian began first grade, at the first parent-teacher conference, I met with his teacher, Mr. Adazio. Every night I came home from work I heard about Mr. Adazio this and that. He was the kids' hero. He was a young attractive guy, a full head of thick curly black hair and a mustache that made his face look charactered, like Clark Gable's did for him. I could see a hell of a build on this guy even through his striped shirt and tie. He had small hands but thick wrists and thighs. He smelled absolutely divine.

About November, talk began about Mr. Adazio's second profession. At first it was just a rumor, that he was stripping at an all male club, and then names and relationships started attaching themselves to the talk: "Judy's brother, who is (whispered) *gay*, went out with a bunch of his (whispered, knowingly) *friends*, and told Judy that it was true. She told me herself!" What would this man do to our students? How could he be a role model when he dances for homosexual men all night?

Jane was outraged and Molly was worried. Marta and Anise just shrugged their shoulders asking, "Who are we to judge?" Before anyone else decided to air out the dirty laundry in a different way, I decided to take it up with the PTA.

I went to the meeting and sat through the regular stuff, statistics on literacy and standardized test results. The addition of a new science teacher for the sixth grade. Et cetera.

"Any other business?" asked the chairperson, a staunch little man named Phil who carried a ceremonial gavel for no apparent reason.

I raised my hand and was called upon. "There is a rumor that Frank Adazio is moonlighting at a male strip club in Tintonville. I believe there is actual witness testimony to this effect." A low tide of chatter billowed up when I first said Frank Adazio. I let the crowd ride it down. "I want to know what you intend to do about it."

Phil pushed his glasses up his nose. "Do you have proof of this alleged second job?"

"I don't, but I believe Judy Grafton does. Judy?"

Judy was a red-faced, small nosed, flat-blue-eyed woman whose chin lay like a pancake on her submerged clavicles. Her breasts and stomach jutted out to the same point, while her atrophied thinnish legs had to be planted slightly farther apart than a normal woman's in order to hold up her midsection. She always looked to me like an egg on toothpicks. Only the egg of her was visible from behind the empty folding chair in front of her as she stood and said, "Yes, my brother saw him dancing at a club called *Jeffrey's*. I know you know what kind of club that is."

Phil sighed. All around me I heard voices filling innocent ears onto the story. I wondered if I could pull this off. All he had to do was ask me what I thought should be done. But I hadn't seen that Frank was there in the audience. He stood next and turned to me with soulful, sad eyes. He looked about to cry. I smiled at him, warmheartedly, trying to convey that it was not in my interest to hurt him. Then he spoke.

"Ms. Eden, you are correct. I have a job as a male exotic dancer on weekend nights. I never discuss my second job with the students and I do my best to see that they understand that I give them as much individual help as they need. And yes, if everyone wants to know, I am...(he breathed) gay. If you think that this somehow interferes with the education of your son, I will resign right here and now. I have been preparing for this moment for a very long time."

I sighed with relief. The whole room was hushed and murmuring. I said, "Well," and the crowd fell silent. "Well," I began again in the silence, "you, sir, are the best teacher I have ever seen in my entire life. I think that the schoolboard must not be paying you enough if you seem to need a second job. I think it would be in the best interests of everyone involved if Phil Robertson here," I gestured with my hand, but did not point, "could approve a raise in your salary that would cover the compensation you get at your second job."

The crowd exploded. Some clapping, some shouting with outrage, some just bewildered. Phil looked back at the principal, Joyce Markham. She cleared her throat trying to gain everyone's attention. When she finally got it, she said, "I think Phil, Karen, Frank and I should discuss this in private. I want to say now that Frank is one of our most esteemed teachers and we will do our best to keep him here, if he wants to stay."

I looked back to Frank, who was smiling. He was a beautiful man, especially when he smiled. Jane glowered at me from nearby and Anise and Marta hugged me. "Good job. Quality work. I haven't seen that kind of educational debate since *Inherit the Wind*." I felt like crying just because I was bursting with all the anger and injustice I had to hold back during the performance. It was, I suppose, like acting when you're playing an evil character and it hurts you to do it. Jane came up to me smiling and said, "ooooh how exciting!"

"I thought you wanted him fired," I said, amazed.

"Nooo. He's not my son's teacher. What do I care?" she added. "That was like a roller coaster ride. I was a little angry at you for not telling me what you had in mind but it was so much fun!"

It didn't feel like fun. It didn't even really feel like victory. When I got home, Julian was waiting for me. Chocolate syrup from a recent bowl of ice cream was smeared across his cheek and his pajamas. The babysitter was asleep. I put Julian to bed and sent the babysitter home and stayed wide awake all night replaying the scene in my head.

What Happened to the Miracle

❖

    Late in August, in the middle of one of the hottest summers Folsom had ever seen, it was terribly hot even at midnight and our air conditioner was not working. Each time I tucked Julian into bed, he returned to the doorjamb of my room, whispering, "Mommy? Mommy?" Finally I put him in next to me. I woke up about eight minutes later in a bed soaked clear through to the mattress. What I thought was the first evidence of a nocturnal bladder problem was just sweat from his damp body making us miserable. I thought about giving him a sponge bath that night, but he was too irritated to take it. Then I remembered what Anise had said.
    I found a pair of swimming trunks for him and we stole through the silent neighborhood. The light of televisions flickered in upstairs bedrooms against the lace curtains, and the street lamps grew to their hottest and fell dark, cycling back to red, white and white hot again, so like eyes that could no longer stand to be open, they closed. I knew that Anise and her family were on vacation in Israel. All the lights at her house were off, but there was a low drone and static of NPR emitting from the basement window. The pool had several prematurely deciduous leaves floating in it, fallen away due to the ecological miscommunication between a short intense drought and our neighborhood sylvan landscape. I touched the water, which was surprisingly cold. Julian sucked his thumb, something he usually only did in his sleep, but his eyes were wide with wakefulness and wonder.
    I had brought swimming trunks for Julian but unwittingly, no swim apparel for myself. I looked into the other empty backyards abutting Anise's property, the low growl and solitary woof of a faraway sleepless mutt was all that it betrayed. I wriggled off my button down cotton nightshirt, stripped down to my panties and hopped into the biting water. My panties quickly oversaturated and allowed water to filter through the low thread count. I was delighted by the way my breasts took on a weightlessness. It felt so natural, and I had never been immersed in water while nude before. At least not since I'd grown breasts. Julian's toes curled around the lip of the

pool and he looked terrified. Before I could say anything, he closed his eyes and jumped into the center, causing a small splash. He sank right to the bottom, four feet down, of the pool. I waited a second to see if he would try to swim, but his body remained motionless beneath the surface of the water. I reached down and fished him up. He whipped his hair out of his face and his terrified arms and hands clutched at my neck. I hushed him and tightened my grip on his body as my feet slipped carefully across the scummy floor of the pool. He was shivering and completely awake.

"Shh," I cooed. "Shh. I've got you."

He watched the forest behind us, and listened to the crickets and the slap of water against water as we moved around.

"Does it feel good?" I asked, but he didn't answer. He shivered against me and visibly grew more terrified. We bobbed around in the water, my silk panties peeling off my ass and Julian weightless against my breasts. Although I held him, I let my fingers run against the soft flesh of my arms and breasts. It was sublime how the skin on my body felt like a custard, like something eggy with vanilla in it, at any rate. I hadn't been touched in five years. I guess that's a long time to go without being used.

He calmed down a little bit since nothing terrible had happened in a couple minutes. His little shivers welled into widely spaced sighs and he stopped trembling as his body adjusted to the cold bite of the water. It was so still, the full moon felt like a night watchman, humble and disapproving, but keeping perfectly quiet. A car passed a block away or so. A cat rustled out of the bushes chasing some unseen smaller creature. She kept perfectly still, glaring at us, sizing us up, and holding her mid-flight pose. I cooed to Julian about the cat, how pretty and mysterious she appeared. We recited a bit of the "Owl and the Pussycat." As we neared her, the cat raced up a nearby sycamore and settled on a sturdy limb. She soon lost interest in us and turned to other, less easily discernible disturbances in the fabric of the night.

"Why don't cats get beds?" Julian asked. His skin had adjusted to the temperature of the water.

"They can sleep anywhere."

"When we go home, I want to sleep outside in a tree."

"You'll fall down," I said.

"No, I'll hold on, like this," he tightened his grip around my neck.

"Should we go home now?"

"No. Walk around the pool three more times." I slid along carefully twice around and heard a half-jangle, half-thud.

"What was that?" I asked aloud to myself.

"Your keys, Mommy," answered Julian and I knew he was right. They must have fallen from the pocket of my night shirt which I had slung over a lawn chair. We took one more turn around, watched the cat hop down from its perch, and then we started out of the pool. A light in the house next door popped on for a moment, and I froze. Julian, however, ran to retrieve my nightshirt. The light popped off.

I hauled myself out of the pool and was stricken by my heft. It was so easy to move in the water, so gentle and warm. I remembered the glory days of my athleticism, my scalp burnt through my sun-bleached hair and my wrists so small I could touch thumb to pinkie circling with each opposite hand. But I remembered I was not happy then, even though I remember being so. I was alone and scared and missing my sister and without freedom. Here I was fat, but happy and free.

I slung the nightshirt over my back and tried to wriggle my wet arms into the sleeves. It was difficult to finagle, but I finally got it on completely, though I'm sure I looked like a finalist at the fatty wet tee-shirt contests they hold at roadhouses. My panties hung low with chlorinated tannic water, and I was not beneath slipping them off and wringing them out, but for the presence of my son. I asked him to turn around and I dropped them to the ground and they hit the floor of Anise's brick patio with a wet smack. As I bent to pick them up, I heard the motor of an approaching car. I raised my head and I saw the wide sweep of red, blue and white lights, the mute herald of the law. The first thing I thought was that someone nearby had died or was in the middle of a heart attack, and it was just serendipity that I would be caught here, now, without panties. Julian ran around upon the stage of the patio back and forth like a monkey trying to figure out what was going on.

"Mom! Can I go see?"

"Stay here!" I hissed, wringing the chemical soup out of the underwear.

Of course, the light. I hopped back into the disgusting wet panties and immediately realized that I should never have removed them. They were slightly twisted since their semi-driedness stuck to my skin at odd angles. Also, the brief respite my butt took during their removal made it difficult for me to stand having them back on. White light from a hand torch exploded from the left side of the house. I pulled Julian to my side and waited for the law. The flashlight found me very quickly and I suppose the cop sized me up quickly as well, as he dropped the mean shine from my eyes.

"G'morning, ma'am," he said. I could see the whites of his eyes flickering in the night.

"Hello, officer."

"I'm sure you have a reasonable explanation."

"Yes sir, I do."

He said something into the fist-sized radio clipped to his shoulder and then, without pad or paper, waited patiently for me to begin. I explained that Anise was a friend of mine and that it was too hot for my son to sleep and that I thought we could just get cool and then go home. Accepting all of this as a reasonable explanation for our nearly naked presence on someone else's property, he said that he would have to escort us home and return to the station. Of course, they would have to alert the Rosens (Anise's family), and if I were telling the truth, no one would press charges.

We started walking with the officer, answering his simply phrased questions, but Julian tugged on the bottom of my sopping wet nightshirt to remind me about the missing keys. I stopped the officer and turned around to retrieve them, but I was completely disoriented by the position of the eight lounge chairs in Anise's backyard. I had no idea which one had held my stuff.

I knew I was straining the cop's last good nerve, but I was desperate. I asked my son which chair the stuff was on. Julian just shrugged.

Even though I had a dandelion-colored rabbit's foot and a bright red environmental thermometer attached to the modest ring of three keys, it took us a full hour to locate the keys, employing the use of his partner's flashlight and both men to search. As the sun climbed into the sky, I thought about how I could brag to the girls about watching the sunrise with not one, but two attractive bachelors, leaving out the grisly details about my own near arrest. The keys had fallen into a clump of grass beneath one of the lounges, and into a rut that had been made by the chair leg's old position. When we got home, I put Julian in bed, where he dropped off to sleep in ten minutes and had completely soaked his sheets again in twenty. I however, replayed the scene in my head, considering the homely but friendly face of the main cop, watching the precipitation of the digital minutes slowly pass until my alarm inevitably went off. The same sun that watched me and my son into the late early morning had hidden himself behind some nice cottony clouds, promising us some much-needed rain.

4. On It Goes

Just after Julian's eighth birthday, my mother and grandmother came over for Thanksgiving, as they did every year. George never saw us anymore because he refused to return to this country. He and his Vietnamese wife wrote astringent letters to my mother, keeping her informed of the names, birthdates and well-being of her four other grandchildren. They never enclosed a mailing address in the letters, so she was unable to reply.

I gave my mother Zeke's Christmas present, which may have precipitated all the giving of Christmas gifts. Zeke is my autistic brother who lives in a care facility in Flowertown, Pennsylvania. Julian and I cannot go see him because he still masturbates whenever he sees me.

It used to happen when I lived in Ohio, and we don't know why me, specifically. He learned how to control his bowel functions when he was four, but whenever I was supposed to help him, he would go right in his pants so I would have to wash them. It happened every single time. My father finally decided that he would try to fix it: whenever I was in charge, my father shadowed Zeke and when he looked like he was going to go, my father would smack him with a belt. Zeke would howl and for a while would go in his pants due to the fear and pain. After about two weeks, he stopped.

But then he discovered masturbation. Zeke used to walk into my room, sit on my bed, back to me, and masturbate. I was sixteen when he was six, but by that time, we knew Zeke was autistic and our doctor told my father that it was because of the beatings and the lack of affection, so what we were supposed to do, according to the doctor, was encourage all kinds of self-expression.

I would not encourage this particular kind of self-expression, so my father would drag him out of my room and sit and watch him and smile and even praise him until he dribbled out his load of semen. Then my father would get him all cleaned up. I left for college the following year, but still whenever Zeke saw me, he would drop his pants, grin and masturbate. He didn't masturbate to anything else in particular. It could have been a bright sunny day on the farm or he might have been playing Frisbee on the care facility's lawn when the spirit moved him, or it might have been at night in the lavatory. I was the only constant, reliable stimulus.

I gave my mother Zeke's gift, which was a new elastic and vinyl netting for a small trampoline. He wore out the ones he had at least twice a year.

My grandmother pointed Julian to his present, wrapped tightly with silver and blue paper that stood uncommitted to any specific holiday. She had knitted him another sailor suit, identical to the five that he had received from her in the previous years. Although she always remembered the pattern down to the slightest detail while she was working on it, she consistently forgot that she had given him the same thing last Christmas, or said she did. Julian smiled and hugged her and my Grandmother looked pleased with herself. She took up her knitting and added a clack-clack-clack to the faraway din of the television in the other room and the sounds of my mother's sighs over my taste, weight or fashion sense. My mother requested that her gift to him remain under the tree until Christmas, and asked me if I had a problem with that. I wanted to spring the Santa gift on him soon, since it was timely and we'd have to prepare ourselves, so I decided that now would be a fine time.

"Hey, Jules," I called to my son, who was folding down the paper that had encased his first Christmas gift. "Santa brought your big present early."

"He did?" Julian scrambled into my lap. "Can I open it now?"

"Sure." I handed him a manila envelope with Christmas stickers all over it. He tore the top off and spilled the contents across the blue berber. "What is it?" I coaxed. "What does it say?"

He spotted the picture on the cover of the brochure of Mickey

Mouse holding a kid's hand in his own and the sprawl of familiar Disney font. "It's a Disney book!" he cried out.

"No, read on."

"He can't read *yet*?" my mother stage-whispered.

"He's getting there," I defended. "Anna May was never a great reader."

"That wasn't my fault."

"You don't have to be here," I warned. "I don't need to take this."

My mother pursed her lips and looked back to Julian.

He had uncovered a blue and white paper envelope that had an airline logo across the bottom and he unfolded the brochure so that its five nested pages were splayed across the floor, a long glossy carpet of gift, shinier than the paper my grandmother had used, but completely incomprehensible to my poor son. He looked up at me forlornly, perhaps hoping that he could just accept the paper as the gift, say thank you and retire with it to another room and make a fort or mosaic with it.

"Sweetie. We're going to Disneyworld!"

"We are?" he asked, wondrously. "Santa got us tickets to Disneyworld?"

"Yes she did." I said. Both of my maternal figures in the room shot me a look. "Look, Ma," I said in my defense, taking on the easier target, "He hasn't got a father. What does he need with a father figure in a big red suit. We got it all worked out here."

Instead of taking me up on the challenge, she went straight to Julian. "So, Julian, can you tell me about Santa Claus?"

"Yes. Santa Claus is a cross-dresser. You can pull on her beard at Macy's because she doesn't have a beard. Girls don't have beards." I looked at him sternly. "But you're not aposed to pull on her beard."

"Did you pull on her beard when you were at Macy's?" I asked him. He nodded shyly. I turned back to my mom. "See, it came up. He asked me why Santa wore a fake beard and I told him."

"Aha." My mother drank her tea. My grandmother, who suffered most of her later life from mild narcolepsy, had fallen asleep. "If I'd known what Santa was getting you two, I might have gotten you something to go with that," my mother slyly vented.

"We could always use upgrades. Santa bought us coach," I suggested. My mother gave a feminine little snort.

Julian looked up to the sky in one of those adorable little moments that make you glad you have a kid, but make you also wonder whether a casting agent for MGM studios is nearby, waiting to step out of the foyer into the living room, remove his hat and say, "Gee, that was great kid, I'm going to make you a star!" Julian said, "Santa always knows just what I want." I flushed with shame for the kid. Here I was, investing all my time and energy trying to teach him discriminating taste and he winds up staring at the ceiling rafter thanking Mother Christmas, a bastardized ideal of a bastardized ideal, for two tickets to Disneyworld. Corporate America, you have arrived.

But I'm crushing dreams, crushing this scene. What can an American kid hope for these days if not some, albeit orchestrated, memorable moments in his childhood? Of course I knew that these happy little bits would be blocked out the next time I grounded him, or when I imposed a curfew or said something wrong.

My mother began her next sentence with "Since...," which is always a very bad sign for me.

"Since you and your son believe that Santa Claus is a woman, and since you have decided to give your presents early and not wait for them to be delivered the morning of Jesus' birth, and since you have turned upside down every tradition that I and your father tried to instill in you..." she waved her hand at our tree, a two-foot potted plant whose banana palm leaves sunk low with the homemade wooden ornaments she'd given us last Christmas. "Since you are the mother and this is your house, I will not try and change anything that you seem to want to ruin. However, I'd like to tell Julian about Christmas when you were all little and what it was like."

I sat back. What I remembered was getting well-intentioned gifts that every kid but me would want. I remember every time I read a word I didn't know in a novel or a textbook that did not have a sufficient glossary, and I couldn't figure it out from context, I would desperately wish for a dictionary. My parents did not have one. We had a thesaurus, a pocket book edition, with several words spelled wrong, and humorously, I suppose, some editor let the word "redundant" in this edition be in the list of synonyms for "redundant." When that joke became popular in the eighties, I just assumed that that comedian had the same thesaurus. Because I was constantly gleaning definitions from the synonyms, I sometimes had a whole string of words misdefined in my mind.

    I received hobby horses and jump ropes, a hula hoop which I could never work, but Anna May took over almost immediately. I received clothing, fashionable, but not as fashionable as Anna May's. She shopped for and paid for her own wardrobe by the time I was paying attention to the clothes on my body. I received an orange in my stocking every year, a clementine. It was a signal of winter, like the appearance of hot chocolate on menus and the sanguine smell of the hissing radiators, iron activated by water, not unlike blood.

    She got me and she knew it. I was faded away in my own sweet nostalgia, hot chocolate and hot blood, the smells rising and mingling in my memory's nose, while she told apocryphal stories of snowmen and snow angels, of babies in mangers and a fat man with a reindeer who had a song. Before I knew it, she had charmed my son, and he was singing the songs with her, having needed a context for the stuff he learned in school. It was all coming at me, I could see it. When would he ask me if Santa was real, when would the innocence be lost? Is there a way to keep your kid innocent without lying to him? Why have we as a culture perpetuated a myth that we all stick to, every adult banded together in a lie that keeps the malls open until eleven and the same songs and school plays and Christmas stuff spinning around and around *ad nauseum*? The answer was on my child's face. He'd crawled into my mother's lap and was smiling, peacefully, happy to know that it was all children that were rewarded on Christmas day, a birthday party for a wonderful little boy, something he could understand without all the truths of history getting in the way.

❖

Disneyworld. I had a team of three of the Junior women swearing up and down that there would be plenty of stuff for adults to do: Paradise Island, perhaps. Jane nodded knowingly, insiderly. She had the feeling that this was where I would meet *the one*. I didn't want *the one* to be from Orlando, and certainly not from any place that wasn't Orlando, and I had a little boy in my room to consider in case I did get lucky. All of this was so foreign to me that it hardly mattered that there would be this sort of seediness, that I could get laid the Disney way. Ha.

We stayed in the Polynesian resort, which was amazingly misty every morning we arose. I almost wondered if the mist was pumped in. When we went to bed, the clean kerosene smell of the burning torches that lit our way was somehow comforting, again in an unsettling, artificial way. There was a place I could drop Julian off and he could watch movies for up to six hours if I wished. I hoped to God there were no children in there, in the dark, watching movies, abandoned, while some set of parents in matching Bermuda shorts snapped pictures of flamingos or sneaked kisses in Epcot Tiananmen Square. I held Julian's hand and swept him through most of the attractions. Neither of us understood Mr. Toad's Wild Ride, but the ride itself was pretty uneventful anyway. I made a note to investigate it for future reading—it looked co-opted, OEMed from an non-Disney affiliate. Perhaps the original would be a good read.

On the second day, after a thorough run around Pioneer Country and a brief trip under the sea (Julian's jaw sat agape the entire time while a steady drip of water amassed and soaked the whole left side of my body), Julian had to go to the bathroom. Because we were at Disneyworld, perhaps, and because it looked kind of eerie, all happy and clean and artificial, I worried about letting him go by himself. He went by himself at home, but at all restaurants and other public bathrooms, he came with me into the women's room. When we stepped into the women's bathroom, a mother who was unbuttoning her blouse to nurse her baby looked up at me and my six-year-old boy in tow unappreciatively. I got the message and retreated into the sunlight. There was a man who tipped his baseball cap at me, a fat cigar like a sixth finger wedged into his sunburned hand. A boy in a red and white striped shirt called out, "hey!" and the man winked at me as if finishing up a conversation. He turned back to the child, which hopefully was his own. I couldn't ignore the glint of gold on his left hand; though I wish I could rid myself of the habit, I'm a ring watcher. Julian was twisting his legs back and forth in a little pee dance and I sent him in to the bathroom alone. His big eyes registered fear at the dark portal that read MEN. Then he steeled up and marched ahead, unbuttoning his pants on the way to the door. I felt slighted that he didn't even wave before he disappeared.

I bit my nails and tried to look casual. I looked at the map, but I couldn't see anything for feeling Julian's absence at my side. *I'm going to be one of those mothers.* I watched the clock, Mickey's gloved fingers barely moved at all. This would be exactly the kind of place to prey upon children, freaks in every bathroom, I thought. My child was going to come out a man. I watched the guy with the glinty gold ring, catching sun at every chance, and I waited for my boy. Finally the woman who had been nursing emerged from the bathroom. There were three girls with her, not including the baby. The woman was much slighter and more hollow than she'd looked in the dark. Her blue veins stretched like cords over her wrists which cradled the child. "Hey, Tom," she called, and Mr. Married came over to take the full, drowsy infant. He looked at me again, his grin wide.

"Come on, ladies." He gathered them together, along with the red shirted boy and another lanky sullen pre-teen. I watched them stop and stand in a ring to read the map. All of them held one arm raised and a finger pointed in a different direction.

A bullish cranky looking man wearing a Stetson and beard headed into the men's room and I stepped back. Then I regretted not asking him to call my son. Now the villain in my fears had a face, girth, a hat. Another looked very clean but was wearing a leather jacket, even though the temperature was fine for sunbathing. The next looked nice, but stopped his wife and said something to her in Spanish, so I just assumed that he didn't know English and bothering him would infuriate his wife. Every man who passed into the bathroom had some defect or something I didn't trust. I wanted some guy to stop his normal wife and kids, someone who called it "a pit stop," or some other cute euphemism. I wanted one like that guy who just left with his tired, nursing wife and seven kids. I should have asked him if I could borrow one of his boys.

I had just seen about five men, all full-grown, none of whom would appreciate my despair, enter the bathroom. Julian had been in there for at least ten minutes and the gang rape scene was really growing more and more vivid in my brain, each churlish pilgrim added to the line, each with his own horrible secret pedophilic desire, waiting for a taste of my son. Like a mother, I burst in and found Julian leaning against the wall, washing his hands with full gobs of white apple-scented soap. I removed him from the bathroom as discreetly and quickly as I could, amidst much grunting and audible petitioning for me to leave. They were just barely watching their language for the sake of my son. I held Julian's arms out in front of him, hoping to keep the white runny goo from slipping down to his elbows before we crossed the eight steps in the sunlight and disappeared into the more hospitable ladies room. We were successful.

"What were you doing?" I asked.

"Nothing. Washing my hands."

"It took you ten minutes to wash your hands?"

He was silent.

"Did you use the urinal?"

He nodded.

"Was it fun?" I asked, genuinely curious. I used to watch my brother pee over fences and write stuff in the dirt or the snow. I was always envious of the ability to use urinals. He nodded and smiled.

"So, kid, what took you so long? No number two..." I tore two paper towels from the dispenser and straightened up as he dried his hands and forearms.

"I was watching them."

"For what?" I asked.

"Their penises. They have big ones. Really big ones." He blinked his eyes and dropped his jaw to illustrate enormity.

"Did you say anything to those men?"

"No," he replied, shaking his head. "I just washed my hands."

"I'll tell you what. We'll do a little investigative reporting on that when we get home."

"What's investive reporting?"

"Research. We'll buy a book."

"A book on penises?" he asked, his eyes growing wide again. He wiped his hands on his overalls. I had my doubts myself.

"We'll find something," I said as we exited into the sunlight, the Disney castle in its indomitable glory striking a rampart into the sky like a beautiful phallic truth, something I'd never ever noticed before.

❖

I remember the first day I took Julian to his first grade, he clutched my hand and was smiling so hard I thought he was going to scream. I had to hold him back to keep him from rushing across the busy street.

"Mommy?" he said. "Who are those children?"

"Those are the other children in the school," I replied.

"Can I go play with them?" he asked, wondrously.

"Of course."

He was friends with every single one of them (except one little Chinese girl who kept forcing herself to throw up) within fifteen minutes. It was inspiring to watch him; my experience was not like his at all.

I had been home schooled, in a way, until I was eleven. At least that's what it said on my parents' taxes. Both Anna May and George had been home schooled until they were ready for high school. At that point, my parents sent them off to the public high school where neither fared very well in their classes, but they suffered no social stigma, as kids came from all over the county and were just meeting for the first time. Neither Anna May nor George was the least bit timid either. It took three months for my parents to decide to put me into a parochial school. I remember being eleven years old and walking in on the first day, my legs cold because of the polyester jumper and knee socks I was wearing. A bunch of girls laughed at me as soon as I came into class and I could see why immediately. There was a necktie that came with the uniform, so I had looked up in the encyclopedia how to knot a tie. I had selected a double windsor and I practiced for hours until it looked correct in the mirror. Every other girl had a low slung plaid bow tie around her neck. A simple bow tie. I tugged at my neck.

"Isn't that nice," said my new teacher, a tall thin Irish woman who, I would learn, liked to play Joan Baez and Joni Mitchell albums during quiet time. "Did your father help you with your tie?"

I didn't answer. The girls laughed some more. I tugged harder, but was unable to undo it since I was no longer in front of a mirror. I remembered that there was a trick, but I couldn't figure it out. The teacher, Mrs. McDonough, whose name everyone but me knew how to spell, helped me loosen it and then retied it so I looked like all the other girls. When I sat down, I heard the girl beside me tell her friend that I might be a boy.

I tried to navigate through the books to find things I hadn't read. There weren't many concepts I hadn't read in another form already. I did have to learn how to diagram sentences and I wasn't very good at converting to the metric system. However, my quiz scores were unfailingly praised by the teacher and scorned by my classmates.

The first three months were like this. I was unpopular, nervous, friendless and smart to a flaw. I gave up. I started going through Anna May's things to find clues on how to handle women, friends, school. I pierced my own ears with some of her small gold studs. Though one became horribly infected, I gained popularity points for my boldness. However, I was called down to the principal's office because of the trend I started. My grades slipped and my circle of friends grew. None of them were really the types of girls that I went to the park or the movies with, the kinds of girls that Anna May used to hang out with and drop fast. They were interested in what I would do next, and characterless on their own. They were all like blank sheets of paper and I was the violent purple sharpie that marked up their worlds. I rewarded those who came up with innovative pranks by carrying them out and often getting caught. My grades were at an all-time low, but only because I had little time for homework.

But when my brother went to Vietnam, my whole life changed. I read the newspaper every day, trying to discern exactly what the America's next move was and what that meant. I studied maps of Asia. I read about Ho Chi Minh, about Buddhism, about Communism, about Socialism. I couldn't have cared less about complex fractions and irrational numbers; I needed tangible facts, I needed to know what it meant to have my brother fighting in a war that it did not seem that we needed to fight.

My pranks dropped away as we watched our older brothers or sister's boyfriends go to war. We whispered on the playground, trying to console each other, trying to understand each other's pain when a brother or cousin or uncle died. But we were eleven and twelve. We were unable to summon the generosity to understand. We were full of hormones and first experiences with menstruation and infatuations with Elvis and the Beatles. It was the scariest, most in-between time of our lives, and we were barely aware of it. I look at my child now, the scariest thing in his world is the computer animated blood in Nintendo games, perhaps a pile-on in the playground. Nothing like what we endured. I wondered sometimes, if he would grow up weak, without the strength to reason what is right and what is wrong. Without opinion. But war doesn't make you have or not have opinions; it just makes you question the existence of God.

Anna May woke me at five o'clock in the morning the day she left.

"Hey Karen," I remember her shaking me lightly. "Are you a good witch, or a bad witch?" she asked, baiting me with a line from one of my favorite movies.

"I'm a good witch!" I said, enthusiastically, perhaps because she was my older sister and still saw me as a child, and perhaps it was because I wanted her to laugh.

"Baby, I'm leaving," she said. "The good news is, all that stuff over there," she dragged her arm through the air less as a sexy sweep introducing the grand prize than as a lazy rake of an oar through still water. "All that is yours. I don't want none of it."

"Where are you going?" I asked.

"You'll see. Don't worry. I promise that you'll see me again, probably on a big screen, and you'll show all your friends that you knew me and that I loved you more than I love anything in the world."

I remember holding her to me, and she smelled like freshly baked angel food cake and a little generically sweet too, like the starch we used in George's collars.

"Can I write to you?" I asked.

"Sure. I'll send an address when I get there. Will you do something for me, baby?" she asked.

"Can I go too? I could be an agent, or I could go with you."

"Baby, you're the only one in this family who is gonna do something with her life. I want you to make sure of that. You stay here for now and when you're old enough, I'll come get you. Then I'll put you through college and you can become whatever you want."

"But you're going to be famous too. I'm not the only one...," I said.

She had a dreamy look, the kind that washed over her sometimes when she talked about a guy she liked or about karma, which she only barely understood. Or the look she had when she dropped acid once and she made me come lie on her bed with her for an hour just running my hands along the fine hairs on her arms.

"Yeah. We're family, baby. I love you so much."

We held each other.

"Okay, but listen. I want you to give this to your mother." When she was fighting with our mother, she would often change the pronoun like that. "Don't open it first, okay? It's between me and her. You gotta live with her for a while, but that's okay. She likes you better. And don't tell Daddy that I left. Even if he asks you, begs you to tell him where I went, don't tell him, okay."

I promised. I promised and crossed my heart.

But less than twenty minutes after she left, the letter to my mother was opened and shoved beneath my mattress into my diary It had been read, re-read and evaluated by my hungry eyes. It was a cruel, uneven letter and there was a threat that should she ever be asked about her family, she would say that she had no mother.

Six hours after Anna May stood, told me that she had changed her name to Miracle, and walked down the blistered craggy road that led to the one bus station in any of the nearby towns, her hair upswept into a beehive, platform boots kicking gray stones into the rutted sides of the long asphalt ribbon, her thick thighs full throttle sixties and sexy, like twin milk bottles that had just a dollop of Hershey's syrup well stirred into them, I was sitting at the kitchen table recounting for the police exactly what she said and wore, how the room looked, where she said she was headed, telling the truth as calmly as I should have been lying, trusting that when she arrived back here within the next twenty-four hours as I was fully expecting her to, she would throw her arms around my neck and tell me how much she missed me and how glad she was to be back that she didn't care that I had told. Seven hours later, on that Saturday, my mother went into an early labor and my father went with her to the hospital. I was left alone with George, to whom Anna May, now Miracle, had not said goodbye. He went outside and threw an old scarred deflated football across half a football field length of our property, and ran to get it. He threw it back to the space he had been standing. He glared at my face watching him through the unshuttered window. I knew he was angry that she had spurned him, but I was calm, knowing that what I had told the police would bring her back, and believing that this was just another episode we all had to live through in order to remain a family.

I don't know whether she knew that I would tell, just from my face that morning. I've never been a good actress. She wasn't on the bus that she had intimated she would be taking. Maybe she went east, to New York city. It seems like it would be easier to get lost there. Our police force filed a report with the missing persons bureau, but nothing ever came of it. She said she was headed to an audition, but that could have been a lie, to throw us off track. Perhaps it was punishment for me, punishment for believing that she wasn't capable of being one step ahead of us, and was able, by fostering a trust between us all those years, to make me believe something deliberately untrue. Perhaps it was her final way of telling me that she wasn't stupid and that, if she wanted to, she could light the whole world on fire.

PART II
A Miracle Lost

5. Pink

When my little angel was old enough to do his own laundry, I taught him how to sort his clothes, read the instructions for temperature and cycle on the lid of the washer, and how much detergent to use. However, sorting by color doesn't seem logical to eleven year old boys; my son ritually sorted all his clothes into two piles - dirty and not dirty. He then hefted armfuls of the dirty clothes into the washer, added a cup and half of the detergent and let it go. As a result, I am proud to report, his karate uniforms came out of the fluff cycle a nice, sugar & spice, pink.

Everyone has pink clothes. Everyone has grayish clothes and yellowed clothes, but I was so proud of my little guy and the soft rosy glow of his *gi* clashing with his hard-earned green belt. During the advancement test there were three rows of the little warriors, and among them, dressed in handicap pink, my boy stood out.

He didn't seem to mind either. He did all the forms beautifully, regardless of his feminine garb, his tar-black soles kicking air and his little fists scrunched up the way they were when he slept right after birth. He was proud - it meant that he could screw up the laundry like an adult male. It was a coming-of-age. Driving home one day, he said to me, "Only men who are comfortable in their sexuality wear pink."

I looked surprised and asked, "And I suppose you are comfortable in your sexuality."

He looked out the window. "I guess so." Then he added, "there's lots of people who are not comfortable in their sexuality."

"Oh, whom for example?"

"You."

"What about my sexuality confuses me?"

"You are just confused," he shrugged. "It's okay. Lots of people are."

"Really? So I'm confused. What am I confused about?"

"Duh…your sex-you-al-ih-tee," I stopped at the red light and looked at him. He made this half-lidded gaping jaw face and drew circles around his ear with his finger.

"That's a pretty big thing. What component?"

"All the components. You don't know who to love."

Could he actually have known what he was saying? Could this little eleven-year-old actually have *meant* to give me this kind of advice?

"Do you mean that I don't know if I should love women or men?"

"No. You always love men. It's just you don't know how to do it right. That's why men don't stay with you. You have to learn that."

"How do you think I got you?"

"What?" This was eleven-year old stalling. He heard me all right, but sometimes he would have this blank stare and said 'what?' in such a dreamy, disconnected way that it could only mean, "I need a second to understand what you just said because that last question did not seem to follow."

"I said, how do you think I wound up with you? You came from a man…"

"I came from a man?"

"I mean, I had to have sex with a man to get you."

"Oh. I know that."

"So obviously, I know what I'm doing."

"But not that kind of sex where you have babies together. Sex where you sleep in the same bed. Sex with *condoms*."

"Oh, right. Sex with condoms. *Real* sex," I said.

Okay, as a mother I'm sure I had the responsibility to set this kid straight, but I don't really know what was wrong with me. It was the same instinct that let him wear the pink *gi* to Karate, knowing that everyone was looking at me like I'm a lazy and pathetic mother because the domestic shit doesn't matter to me. I told myself that he would have more lasting information if he figured it out for himself, and if he trusted me not to baby him, to let him learn at his own rate. That was all bullshit. It was the instinct that intrinsically gets a kick out of what he was going to come up with next, the instinct to humor him and to hope he gets something out of having a mother like me.

I remembered how kids talked about stuff they didn't know anything about. I remember girls as school professing their knowledge about sexual relations, pretending to fake orgasms, talking about the proper procedure for enticing a boy to make love to you. We would have playground sessions of show and tell, sneaking in smutty books or pictures and forming a circle around them in the yard, oohing and ahhing until a teacher would investigate. I remember reading in one of our pilfered stroke mags about a "Hawaiian Muscle Fuck." This is where the man puts his penis between a woman's breasts and has sex with her that way. We didn't understand that you had to move back and forth at that time. We all thought that it was as easy as fitting a pencil into a pencil sharpener and something inside our vaginas was going to do something as dramatic to a man's penis as the sharpener did to your fresh new number 2 Faber-Castell. And we couldn't wait to get breasts because it determined your sexual prowess, although the correlation of breast size and sex remains a mystery to me even today.

I was eleven once. I figured I knew how he knew about condoms.

"What are condoms, anyway?" I asked.

"Yuck! You don't know what condoms are? All grownups know what condoms are..."

"Humor me."

"You put them on your penis when you want to have sex." Good so far.

"Why?"

"Because you can't have sex without them," he ventured. That was good enough for me.

"That's true," I said as we rounded the turn into our development.

Suburbia always looks so green to me. It's like a permanent movie set. Where I grew up, grass was gray-brown until it died and covered over with snow. It was a lush, pretty world here. More than a few people were out pushing baby carriages and two boys had set up a lemonade stand but I was unhappy to notice that the sign, with its rustic backwards L, and stand were store-bought. Worse, when we stopped to buy some, we were told that they were not selling any—they were just "playing Lemonade Stand."

When we turned into our driveway I noticed Julian's swing set tire had been stolen. We had been warned about this. Apparently the neighborhood teenage boys play a game called "I want" after midnight wandering around in past-curfew impermeable broods that would spy something on a lawn, say "I want," indicating the object, go to great measures to acquire it, and then drop it, saying, "I don't want anymore" when they lost interest, usually a couple doors, but often several blocks, away. There had been an article in the newspaper about the game (the local news took it as seriously as a serial murderer) and there had been a section of the classifieds added, squeezed in between the prayers to St. Jude and the Obituaries, called "I Want Back." The tire was pointless since I could easily get a cheap one from a junkyard, but it enervated me. I felt outwitted and undone.

❖

Of course, I did not plan Julian. He was a product of that one night that my dishes clattered to the ground before Abraham ran off to pick his wife and child up at the airport and left me to deal with the mess. He was a true love and then a true hate. I did it all completely wrong: he was the first man who ever seemed truly interested in me; he was my boss; and he was married. Three strikes against the little worm that planted itself in my belly. His wife found out about me and came to tell me what a bitch I was. She actually meant to stick a little note under my door but coincidentally I was just taking the garbage out by the curb and I found her. Her tiny little figure was shivering, kneeling there. She was wearing, of all things, a sky blue bikini, and her hair, long and black, was wetly matted to her head and back. She had a Walkman on and I could hear the samba music from three feet above her little ears.

She dropped the note which was a folded, surprisingly heavy bond white A3 page full of terrible spelling and punctuation. It didn't matter to me at that point—I'd already missed two periods and quit my job. I was ready for the next part of my life.

I only started working again after Julian was born—I didn't want to risk anything working while pregnant at the plant. In the biochemical field you can't be too careful. A woman I knew one day was feeling nauseous and she left early to drive over to the health center. She was found dead in her car that evening, and the autopsy results were never released to the employees. There's a rumor that the Geiger reading in her lab was way over the risky mark, so I didn't want to take any chances while pregnant, even though the sequencing labs, where I spend most of my time, are pretty safe.

I worked at that plant for three years and moved to a new facility when we moved to Folsom. I kept to myself mostly at the new site. My boss was a woman and I had an everchanging lab full of enthusiastic college interns to initiate and instruct. I had been there about eight years when I was put in charge of a skinny, careless lab tech who ruined an eight month report while performing a routine simple titration. He had gone to have a cigarette and locked himself out of the lab the night before, so he missed the readings. As punishment, and to get myself out of a situation where I could say things I didn't want to say, I took a cigarette from his pack and I went out to the courtyard. As weird as it seems now, I had never left my building from the back in the middle of the day. When I had to take Julian to the doctor, if I couldn't schedule an appointment at night, I left from the front. It shocked me that so many other scientists, mostly women, stood next to the doorway and smoked all day long. They sighed every time someone opened the door and she or he let out a little of the precious air conditioning to cool down the group. One man was telling a story and gesticulating wildly with his hands. Swirls of smoke wafted around the group like an insistent magic trick. I moved past them quickly, not because the smoke bothered me, but because they seemed close-knit and suspicious. The women had brought their purses out with them and kept them tucked beneath their arms, and the men didn't make eye-contact. I felt like I was infiltrating.

A few construction workers were milling about the courtyard working on building a new parking deck. One beefy guy with square brown glasses and a reddish mustache sat near me.

"You got an extra cigarette?" he asked.

"No, I borrowed this one."

"Well I'll just take that one then," he said and stretched out his palm. I felt my jaw drop open and he retracted his paw and said, "Nah, I'm just kidding." He smiled a row of shiny not-too-white teeth.

"Good one," I looked away. But then, for some reason, I looked back. He was wearing cufflinks, small ones, diamond-shaped platinum. He wore them on the cuffs of a clean but worn, blue pin-striped button down shirt tucked into faded jeans. The cufflinks were almost anachronous. Or maybe the jeans were. He was still beside me, wanting a cigarette, staring out and filtering the sun with only his light red lashes and the softly furry Irish brow. His smell was gruff but clean, like fresh motor oil, and his skin was insistently pink. His eyes were terribly light, like water in a glass, and he never seemed to settle into just looking at one thing, but huffed and changed positions and still dissatisfied, huffed and shifted again.

Finally he blurted out, "Did you know that women whose husbands smoke have a much higher chance of contracting breast cancer?"

I laughed.

"I was taking a chance there," he said.

"Oh, I don't get offended easily."

"No, I mean I didn't know if you'd get it."

"I got it."

Then he told me a story about a ten-inch pianist.

Then he told me about his wife who wouldn't have sex with him and he didn't know why, and then he told me about a woman in his neighborhood who wanted him to have sex with her but he didn't want to cheat on his wife. Then I just gave him my cigarette and tried to go back inside.

"Hey, you know, I'm not a nut case," he implored. The cigarette

was tiny in his thick callused fingers. He rubbed his cheeks with his free hand.
"I know."
"Do you wanna get a beer later?" he asked.
I honestly had not been asked to do something social with a man since Abraham, Julian's father. I wanted a beer. I wanted to be shown the places I could not go by myself. I wanted an adventure, and sure, what the hell, I wanted to help this man through his marital problems. I didn't know any solutions, but it didn't matter. I said yes, and when I got back to the lab, I impulsively ran my fingers through the lab tech's hair, smiling at my good luck. I think he was just glad I wasn't pissed off anymore.

Our first beer was at what became our regular restaurant and bar and he told me jokes and stories about the time he spent in jail when he still did cocaine. (He told me about the frayed edges of a world that defined itself with isolation and need. I understood; I smiled.) I told him about Julian and Barnesville. His wife asked for a separation. He taught my son to play the saxophone and how to read Braille (his mother was blind). We would talk until it was too late for him to go home. Soon the fold-out couch in the basement was replaced by a bed and we had a pretty permanent roommate.

He bought a cat for Julian's eleventh birthday. Julian named her Slanky and she brought presents of the rodent and small bird variety for us. Bruce and Julian created a trophy case from a pilfered test-tube rack using coffee stirrers as stakes and we set the tiny skulls on top. We nailed the display two feet over the cat dishes and Slanky seemed to be happy enough with our handiwork. When Bruce's truck broke down, I drove him in my Volvo. When my Volvo needed repairs, he took me in the truck. It was like a live-in carpool, a relationship of convenience. He made me laugh.

One night, about a year after he moved in with us, after I'd put Julian to bed, Bruce lay down on his back on the kitchen floor.
"It's official today," he sighed.
"What?"
"My divorce. It's all over."
"Really? So what does that mean?" I asked. I took two

McDonald's glasses from the cabinet in order to pour a toast.

"It means that I don't have a wife. It means I'm free." He looked at me. "But I'm not lonely."

"Cheers," I said, lowering a glass of wine to his hand and slumping myself to the floor beside him.

"You know, next to bowling, you're the thing I love most in the world," he said.

"Bowling?"

"Yeah, actually—next to bowling and a little more than Julian." I drank my toast.

"I think I love you, is what I'm trying to say." He took off his glasses and rubbed his brow with the back of his sleeve. I sat down on the floor beside him.

I didn't need him. I don't need him. I could do this without him. Julian and I were fine. And I was not aching to share my bed or my bank account or to bother opening my legs to him. I made it through nine months of pregnancy alone, Lamaze class alone, headaches, backaches and fatigue alone. I drove myself to the hospital. I called my mother after I delivered Julian, a fat yellow cherub of nine pounds. Her answering machine clipped to a dead circuit before I could relay the news. When Julian came I had something to do, someone who loved me and needed me desperately. But this guy had a past, a history, an ex-wife.

Now I had a big, sweaty guy on the floor of my kitchen, and yes, I was in love with him, but I didn't know what I wanted to do.

"Bruce?"

"Yes, Karen?"

"You don't bowl. I've never seen you bowl. You have never bowled, as far as I know." I said.

"I guess that makes you number one."

I put my legs across his chest and drank the wine. I rested my head against the cabinet and when I opened my eyes, I saw he was dead asleep, peaceful, furry and pink under the fluorescence of the overhead lamp, as comfortable on the linoleum as he had been in jail, in the basement, on the floor when he lived with his wife and in the bathtubs he'd passed out in during his life. He was a man used to hard things, hard floors, hard hits. He'd found a home here. I pushed one of my warm socked feet against his cheek to remind him that he was welcome.

❖

Julian fell asleep watching the late movie with me one night. He was emitting a low wheeze with every exhale due to the vestiges of a cold, and I was feeling pretty sleepy, but somehow too irritated to rest. Whatever channel we were watching announced commercial breaks with a bleating trumpet that seemed several decibels louder than the drone of the actors and the soundtrack of the movie. Julian shifted each time the trumpets blared before some perky woman or child attempted to convince me to purchase dog food or whitening toothpaste. My hand was stretched over the edge of the couch, Julian's twelve-year-old head on my arm, and my hand abutted the cold plaster wall. There was a scrap of paper on the floor I hadn't noticed before, and my attention shifted to that. As an apparent bruise grew in magnitude on my contorted arm and Julian's wheeze and the trumpets and wide-eyed women with bobbed hair attacked my nerves, I became preoccupied with trying to discern what the paper was, its origin, and why it had not made it the extra foot into the trash can that sat recently emptied next to the couch. I reached the arm that was not caught, but fell short by more than a foot. I stretched my leg and kicked it slightly further. I peeled one of my socks off with the toes of the other foot. Julian shifted. His whistling was so annoying that I almost wanted to wake him up, or hold his nose, or pry open his lips a little so the air would be redirected. A white haired woman on television was demonstrating the positions of her adjustable bed. I got the paper and drew it to me, and, stretching, reached my good hand to my prehensile, but now chilly, toes to gather the spent page. It was a receipt for a book I had bought the week before. I looked at Julian and he whistled softly, imperfectly, blissfully unaware of how insane he was driving me.

I put the receipt in my tee-shirt pocket and brushed Julian's sweaty hair from his forehead. He smelled like warm milk. Slanky jumped up on our legs and nestled himself a warm comfortable space between my shins, his front legs resting on Julian's calves, and slowly kneaded his paws into the blanket we wore. The movie went on, "Merry Christmas, Bedford Falls!" Jimmy Stewart called out. It was lightly snowing out the window, not unusual for Folsom in November. I heard Bruce downstairs in the basement, probably believing that I was asleep. I thought he might be working out with weights since he was groaning and grunting, but what I heard was the one thing I wasn't giving him. He was a man, after all, and sure, upstairs in my bedroom I was guilty of the same furtive measures. I'm sure Julian would be soon hiding in the bathroom, and a couple more years, wet sheets. It was happening to all of us—we were living our sexual lives alone, behind closed doors, aware of the familial love we shared but refusing to call ourselves a family, and aware of the needs we had, but so used to taking care of ourselves, we didn't trust each other with our bodies.

In Barnesville, the sound of my mother and father making love was not natural. One never heard my mother, but my father wailed, like a long exhausting lament. The bed creaked and the floorboards in our rickety house shook. I was instilled with a fear of sexual relations perhaps by the dangerous quaking of the desperate old house, or maybe by the confrontation of my mother's face in the morning, sour and mean, and stoicness of my father's face, always the same, no more or less relaxed for the wails and the cries that had kept us up all night.

I was frozen in place and I heard Bruce making love to himself, getting what he could out of his neglected body. I looked down at the wedge of my body, long neglected as well. I was ugly and fat. I was thick and shapeless and I was sweaty and crude. I dared not breathe during the muffled ritual, the sounds making their ways up the stairs. I wished I could hold him and tell him it was okay to do this, that I was glad of the thinness of the living room floor, that had I known, I would let him do it in my own bed, so I could share it, so we could consummate our humanness, swear to love each other, reject the inherent shame, learn how to physically love another person again.

All became silent and the credits of the movie climbed across the screen. The snow was silver in the light of the television. It was so peaceful outside. I breathed again, and Julian moved to a position that relieved the whistle of his errant nostril. I heard Bruce's heavy step on the stairs and I closed my eyes. I heard the door open gruffly and then quiet. His body moved slowly past our seemingly sleeping bodies stretched across the couch, our ears only a couple feet from the hollow of the stairwell. I heard the refrigerator open and I knew he was drinking orange juice from the carton. He coughed, quietly, loosening phlegm. Water ran and stopped. His footsteps neared and stopped at the edge of the living room. I deepened my breathing to suggest sleep and I heard the familiar sound of his hand brushing the reddish stubble on his cheeks. He came closer and I was terrified that he was trying to discern whether we were asleep. I flinched before I realized that it was his fingers on my forehead and tried to cover up my wakefulness by snuggling into Julian. His palm pressed down on my cheek and his lips touched my forehead.

I felt the cat be lifted off of my shins, then Julian lifted off of my arm. He held my cold hand before bringing it down to the couch. Then he tucked Julian back into my body and I was much more comfortable than before. The cat was replaced and my forehead was kissed again. The television turned off and it was a weighty silence, wearing Julian's rapid, young slight wheeze and my false sleeping breaths. I heard him move to the window and him sigh calmly. I peeked in the darkness.

He had his left hand on the sill and was looking outside at the snow. His fingers were spinning something flashy and gold around, the eerie silvery white of the snow illuminating it, catching light. It was his ring, his wedding ring. I found it in the soap dish once, and again in my camera bag. Each time I returned it, he slipped it into his pocket as if it were his dirty underwear or something he wanted to take care of himself. This is what he misses: this quiet after-sex time. Or maybe it's part of a ritual of purging, maybe something he started way back when they stopped having sex, when he had to start caring for himself, start looking inside to see what went so very wrong and his only answer being, *something in me, but something unfixable.* I remembered my father's wails and my mother's silence, and I thought about his body touching mine. I shivered with that terror of distrust and pain of desire that a body gets from considering something dangerous. Bruce turned to me and I shut my eyes.

"Karen?" he asked.

I didn't answer.

"Karen, come on," he said. I opened my eyes.

He came to the sofa and knelt down in front of us. "You know, I'll always be there for you. You and Julian," he said. I nodded. He was no longer holding the ring.

"I know," I said.

"And I'm going to make him into a football player; the kid's all flab," he said.

I chuckled, as softly as I could. Then I said, "Like his old mother."

Bruce smiled sadly. "Hell, I'm no influence!" he said a bit too loudly and grabbed a bit of his belly. Bruce hushed himself as Julian shifted into my shoulder.

"We're a family," I said. He looked slightly taken aback and looked past me into the wall. I swallowed the lump rising in my throat because of the way I was talking and lying on the couch. He nodded without looking at me and then turned his eyes back upon me and Julian.

"I would like that. I would like to be part of one again."

"Me too."

Julian's eyes opened and closed briefly. His eyes opened again and he blinked twice. Then he settled back to sleep.

"Good night," I said to Bruce. He kissed me on the lips and I lost control of my breathing.

"Good night," he said and stood up. He blew me a kiss before heading back down the stairs.

I didn't fall asleep that night at all.

6. Underwear

Julian's body, in one year, stretched from a flabby five-foot-seven to a gangly athletic six-foot-two. I knew it was my family's genes finally making their appearance. He was George's size, one inch shy of my father's final height. Abraham had been barely taller than I was; he stood five-eight in boots. Julian ached all the time, and ate even more often. His voice took about three weeks to deepen and girls noticed immediately. As we walked together through the mall, he would turn his head and clear his throat to cause gaggles of teen queens to roll with laughter. He put up mirrors all over his bedroom.

He and his friends went for a night out at the hockey rink, chauffeured by Bruce, allowing me time to paint my toenails and pluck my eyebrows. The troupe of them came back to the house and draped themselves around the living room as I was letting a face mask dry. They let the TV play reruns of The Real World as they commented on new movies and new bands and new couples at their high school.

After taking their company for a while, I decided to wash the green mask off my face. As I climbed the stairway I heard a very slight thump come from Julian's bedroom, as if a lamp tumbled from his nighttable. I waited frozen on the stairs to listen for more sounds. Nothing came, so I climbed again.

I carefully approached Julian's room, as if I were walking along a dangerous ledge. My heart was pounding. Could it be a burglar who had sneaked in behind the troupe of kids? I thought of that urban myth that circulated when I was little about gypsies who broke in during parties at your house and made off with your things. Perhaps it was an errant drug-addicted friend? A long slim line of light let in from the hallway into his room and traced the edge of Julian's awful *Victoria's Secret* models poster. All that was visible was a glossy shock of blond, a perfectly circular mole on a slice of pink cheek, and the heft of a breast as it rose from the lace trimmed boustier.

I swung the door open and beheld two high school freshmen. The boy's name was Jimmy and he was a classmate of Julian's, an after-school sometime buddy. I had not met the girl before. Her brown and black sweater was pulled up over her head, trapping the rest of her arms and ponytail, and her bra was unsnapped in the front. Her skirt was up over her hips and the tops of her thighs sported garters but no panties to match. Her lips were smeared across with a mulberryish color and she was flushed, partly from embarrassment, but no doubt from the adolescent ecstasy Jimmy had promised her, and had fully intended to deliver. His Oxford shirt was open to an unimpressive milky chest with precious few hairs and his pants were around his knees. His sweet sheepish brown eyes ringed with forgive-me lashes stared at me bewildered by my presence and then his teeth gave way to the only remaining argument for this situation, "Oh, I didn't hear you."

I told them to get dressed. However, I noticed, as he twisted around to try to discreetly pull up his pants, that the underwear he wore had in block letters my son's initials along the waistband. I had magic markered it on there *specifically* so this would not happen. This, above many other things, really pissed me off. How can a boy put on underwear that is so obviously not his own? How can he miss such overt markings? And I was really specific when I picked out those shorts. I got the all-cotton type, and made sure that the elastic was tough. They were fifteen dollars a pair and never seemed to go on sale, and for all I knew they'd traded in a locker room at gym and my son had put this boy's smelly butt-sweaty shorts on and now I had a migrant polyester blend in the dormant load of whites in the downstairs hamper.

There was really nothing I could do—I could offer to trade him another pair of underwear, but that would defeat the purpose. Then it came to me.

"Take off those underwear."

"What?" he asked.

"Take off your pants and then the underwear. I want those underwear back. They belong to my son."

"Ms. Eden, it's freezing outside!"

"Strip." I commanded. The girl had snapped her bra back in place and was wriggling her sweater down. When she was completely reassembled I dismissed her. Her fists still clenched the bottom of her skirt as she ran off to the bathroom, no doubt to expel what had built up in her bladder from the sight of me. The boy took his pants off slowly and gave them to me. Then he turned his body around and slid the underwear to the floor. His ass was scrawny and had a couple pimples.

"Okay," I rushed into my bedroom and tossed Julian's underpants onto my bed. I retrieved a pink pair from my lingerie drawer and came back into Julian's room. "Wear these instead." I could see my reflection in the mirror, crusty green flakes were peeling from the sides of my mouth and the whites of my eyes looked yellow because of the mask and the lighting. Holding out the candy-colored panties to an unwilling, red-faced boy, I looked like some evil genie in a school play commanding my charge to do my laundry.

"But..." He held his wrists in front of his pubis and shifted from foot to foot.

"I have your pants now. Put on the underwear or you're going home exactly like I found you here." Green flakes wafted onto the chest of my bathrobe as I spoke.

He stepped into the underwear and feigned some sort of debility by losing his balance.

"They're regular underwear. Just put them on." I was losing some patience. But I have to say I was quite amused.

His half hard penis pressed against the pink silk like the nose of a pickled embryo smooshed up against the wall of its jar. My size sixteen hips had stretched out the panties and the sides hung slightly limp on his bony frame. I tossed him back his pants and washed off my face.

I waited for him to dress and I followed him down the stairs. All the kids had their jackets on and the closet girl was shivering. She'd reapplied her lipstick though.

"Leaving so soon?" I asked. All the kids were nervous and looking at the floor, except some kid with tortoise-shell glasses and huge teeth who was slowly snapping up his jacket but kept missing the snaps because he was still watching TV. And Julian, who was staring at me in horror.

"Hi, kids," I said, genially. The girl dropped her head so far to her chest that her hair covered her face entirely. Julian shot me a look that told me how much I had just embarrassed him. I checked for guilt, but there was none, as far as I could tell. I was quite proud of myself. My face burned a little and felt very tight, but that was because of the mask.

"Fine. I'm going to bed. Good night." I beamed.

"Good night Ms. Eden," chimed the buck-toothed kid, with decreasing cadence and conviction as he heard his own voice solitary among the non-existent chorus of good nights. He found only downcast eyes as explanation.

About two months after that fiasco, Bruce called me from a job site in Connecticut to tell me that he wanted to take me away for a weekend.

It meant sex. It meant romance. It meant that he wanted to take me away from the family thing we were doing, and onto a date. It meant a major shift in our relationship, but it didn't bother me. Even though he was stuttering trying to convince me that it would be up in the Berkshires in Massachusetts and it was a nice place and that he had a buddy who had a house, it felt natural. So I laughed. It made no sense—I had a mental cartoon of his burly body sweeping me off my feet, my hair thrown back and luxurious curls dripping off my head and my long arm outstretched holding a gold card out to a bowing maitre d'. He was up for it, I was up for it. I laughed and said, "yes, yes, yes."

As Bruce recounted stories that the construction guys had been sharing, I twirled the cord of my phone around my fingers as if I were a teenager. I lay back on my bed and stared at the ceiling, dreamy, happy. I heard myself giggling. Then I caught my reflection across the room.

I was too fat to be romanced, I determined. I had no sexy underwear, and even if I'd had any, I would have looked horrible. I would have had to wear one of my velour robes, since it was going to be cold. I became instantly terrified.

Everything on me felt bloated and tired. Chunky, as my mother loved to call it. I was trying to listen but I was preoccupied with the amount of ripples my belly made when I tapped it.

"What's that sound?" he asked.

"Huh?"

"That thwack-thwack-thwack sound."

"Oh—I'm just smacking my belly to watch it wiggle."

"Hm…that's pretty sick, babe." Again, I giggled. I watched myself giggle. I was forty-one years old and I was giggling. It was not a pretty sight.

Bruce and I had maintained platonic relations up to now—a miracle in itself, since we had occupied the same space for over three years. He was my tenant in a way, and he was slowly and tentatively becoming my lover.

"So we're leaving on Friday morning. That doesn't give me much time to set the lookout on Julian while I'm gone."

"Let the kid have some fun. House parties are a teenage rite of passage. I had plenty when I was a kid."

"Not in this house. We have several rites of passage, like sharing a beer with your mom or making your own dinner."

"Ah, you're a boring mom. I think I'll bring home a six-pack for the kid."

"I think he'd rather have chocolate syrup for his milk."

"You don't think he's ever even tried drugs?"

"When he was nine I found him trying to snort Luv-My-Carpet, but then we had our drug talk and now I just don't think he's interested. He's less curious than I was back then. Kids these days just seem *cleaner*."

"But that's healthier; they don't fight like boys did when I was a kid."

"I guess it must be easier for him than it was for us. Growing up, I mean."

"There was that underwear thing…"

"Experimenting. Let them experiment."

"When did you lose your virginity?" I asked him. He sighed in response.

"Do you really want to know?" he asked me.

"Yes, of course."

"I was twelve. With the babysitter."

I thought about Jennie, the twenty-year-old blonde who sat for Julian from the time he was eight. She quit last year.

When I was twelve, sex was the furthest thing from my mind. I wanted love and to be loved and to be married. I knew about sex, but I knew about sex in a very natural animal husbandry way. I never considered that people could do such things. I think I even still believed in Santa Claus. It scared me that girls wore makeup in Julian's middle school and that the boys were cultivating a boyspeak that was worthy of a high school gym locker room. I could practically smell the hormones that hung in the air surrounding the group of his friends.

"Look. It's only three days. What's the worst thing that could happen?" Bruce's rumbly voice asked across the hundreds of miles of fiber optic wire. I wondered, crossed my fingers and hoped for the best.

❖

I was terrified. My legs ached from tension and expectancy while we drove to the house. Bruce kept giving me little knowing stares and calling me "babe." I knew he was excited and he sang every song that came on the radio.

"It's okay, babe. You're doing great, babe," he kneaded my thigh as he reassured me and then sang the next chorus of "Comfortably Numb."

I didn't feel great. I was exhausted and spring was starting later more north. We drove way beyond the limestone green spring buds and cool, wet moss, that promised new stuff and back into the last two weeks of hard, cold winter. Snow lay on the banks of the highway median strip and the trunks of the trees looked more stark and starving and dead. The grass looked like resistant stubble on a soap caked leg. I could smell New England's just-spring smell even through the closed windows. Drawn down my right leg was a line of a very slight discomfort—the kind that can't decide whether it wants to be numbness or pain.

I was watching out the window so long at the changing landscape and thinking so hard that I hadn't noticed we'd gone so far out of our way that the road in front of us, no longer a sure and comforting one- or two-digit highway, was about to abandon its pavement entirely in about three hundred yards. There was a curious yellow sign that alerted us to a very ambiguous END, but I could not figure out what was ending. Not the end of the road, since the road carried on *in spirit* for much longer beyond this sign. Long, snowy trenches dug with truck tires and chains ran out and disappeared, pinched away by the overtaking snow. Maybe it was the end of civilization, or maybe the sign was to mark where the state had run out of asphalt for this particular road. Bruce's cheeks were a terrible red as he recognized the fatality of this route.

I decided that the sign actually designated the end of your driver's temper because Bruce simply and eloquently punctuated the last expense of his patience with, "I give the fuck up."

Bruce smacked the steering wheel twice on the right, jarring the windshield wiper switch into the furiously ON position. As the wipers screeched across the glass, he smacked the left side, and then did the right one last time. His last frustrated whack broke off the plastic end on the tube that carried the signal to the windshield wipers. Red and blue wires streaked with white poked out of the stump like an incestuous brother vein and sister artery. Bruce screeched to a stop just at the edge of the unroad and gaped at the damage. I reached over and turned the key a half-turn leftie loosy in the ignition and hushed the motor. The wipers froze midsweep. I lifted my hand up between us in a sort of half stop and half offer. He gaped. I gulped reflexively. He turned his eyes to my hand and stared at my palm trying to discern meaning, guidance.

I moved my hand to his face and his eyes closed. I brushed my palm along his bristly cheek. His great paw came up and drew my hand to his lips, and he kissed my palm deeply. His other hand scooped around the back of my head and we kissed. It was a lovely kiss. I could smell his shampoo and his personal smell which was exuding from his scalp and also the orange peel that I had tossed the floor behind my chair. I breathed in deeply, and he jammed his entire tongue into my mouth.

I froze. He held my head to his mouth and I felt like I was about to be eaten. He let go and looked at me and his hand dove down between my melting thighs and found the lace on my new panties and the soul of him took over the character of his face; I swear I watched him fall in love with me. I demurred. He sighed, smiled and restarted the car. He made a wide U-turn and quickly retrieved our abandoned interstate. Divinely guided, he navigated us pretty much directly to a bed & breakfast perched on the corner of Route 2. I had to say, I was happy to stay at a B & B and eschew the trip to the "friend's house." At least here I knew the sheets would be clean. The sun even came out, that's how perfect it all was.

We crunched into the asphalt driveway, and though I maintained a low level of the terrific fear generated from the last episode, I was mainly cheerful. Bruce was whistling, "A Foggy Day." I stared out at the sunset past the trees. We were situated on a slope of a mountain and the sun dipped below the pines and firs on a sister peak. The snow struggled to maintain its whiteness using an insistently glistening sheen of ice, but the navy blue swathe of the sky was encroaching and the white was a half-light gray with sparkles. Bruce stopped whistling.

"Hey, could you grab that one?" he called. He was more bag than man, the entirety of our luggage strapped to him except one paper bag left in the trunk. He clenched my purse in his left hand. I took the paper bag and closed the trunk with a satisfied vacuum sucking sound that only luxury cars have. He grinned and held out my purse.

"Gimme that!" I smiled. I pulled it too hard and set him off balance, but he stepped forward to right himself.

"You're a very silly man."

"You'll need your strength."
"Promise?"
"Guarantee." I smiled like a schoolgirl, had I ever been that kind of schoolgirl.

We opened the large oak door of our room to twin poster beds dressed with white jacquard bedspreads with a Victorian doll perched upon each one. One bed faced us and the other was sideways along the far wall. It was unsettlingly similar to the room I'd stayed in when I visited my grandmother when I was a child, which had once been my mother's room. I lay down on the sideways bed and stretched out; the mattress felt like the one I had slept on, stuffed with buckwheat and unnaturally convex with very little give. Along the ceiling ran a long crinkle that halted about a foot from the ceiling fan. I closed my eyes while Bruce struggled with the heavy iron frames, trying to shove them together to make a double bed.

"Fuck." said Bruce.

"We're just going to have to snuggle," I offered, teasing.

"Look at you..." his face broke into warmth. "You look so at home here. You look so pretty with these flowers behind you."

I looked around to see what he saw. Maybe he did know me. Maybe I wasn't the really independent woman he'd always known me as. I actually had to reevaluate for myself whether I liked this stuff underneath it all. He sat down on the bed next to me and moved my wayward hair from my face. He was really happy. It was easy taking off my sweater and jeans, and of course he stripped down easily, but I locked as he tried my blouse. I couldn't ask him to turn off the lights because the sun was pouring through the windows. I was hoping to delay him through the sunset so he didn't have to see me.

He kissed me and touched my breast through my gargantuan D-cup triple-ply cotton bra. I had a flashback to me facing myself in the JC Penney dressing room, my shoulders thrown back trying to minimize the pockets of flab squishing out from my armpits. I saw my disappointed face and how naked and mashed and white I looked. I chose this bra because it held me in best. It held my breasts above my stomach, creating a short isthmus between my breast fat and stomach fat. Sitting, however, I knew the two met in large rolls. I was just about to cry, but the tears hadn't eked out yet, so I stopped him.

"Let me give you a blow job." It was all I had. I couldn't let him touch me and I was thinking about that old joke about a short woman with no teeth. It wouldn't matter what I looked like.

"You want to?" he asked.

"Yes." I touched his denimed crotch. There was a sort of familiar bulge that terrified me. Guys used to call it wood, or a hard-on. I'd heard Julian and his friends call it a chubby and a fatty. I didn't need to think about that right now.

He pulled me on top of him. I kissed my way down to his crotch and extricated his penis. His underpants were baby blue. I closed my eyes and did what I remembered. He moaned and lolled about and I really began to enjoy hearing him moan, knowing that it was because of what I was doing. I looked up and found the reddish hair around his navel endearing and when I lifted my eyes up more, I could see his lips, pursed and red like a sweet cherry gumdrop, caught in the peach and lemon fuzz of his beard. He was perfectly vulnerable, all mine. I worked harder and closed my eyes again. His hands flailed around on the bed, grabbing the pillows and the sheets.

And then he sat up.

His hand reached to my neck and I was terrified that he was going to choke me, but instead he took hold of my shoulder.

"Owwwuhhuoww..." his other hand fled to his left temple.

"What's wrong?" I sort of choked on spit, so I coughed.

"My head really fucking hurts."

I swallowed the spit and stopped coughing. "Do you want some aspirin?"

"Yeah. Maybe. I don't know."

"What happened?" I asked.

"I don't know."

"Can I get you anything?" I was desperate. Though I was riddled with concern, I concealed my stomach fat with a layer of bedsheet. Maybe, I thought, he pictured me naked and something stopped the blow job process for him. Maybe I bit him. Maybe I was just very *bad*.

"I think I want a shower."

He didn't look okay. He was flushed, but he was always flushed. He kept his eyes low and the light in the room had faded to a pre-twilight gray. His body was broad and flat and I realized that we hadn't even really gotten him undressed. He stood and, teetering, delicately extracted his thick ankles from each of his pant legs.

"Should I come with you?" I asked, knowing he'd refuse. I couldn't possibly get naked now.

"Nah. I'll be back in a second."

While he was gone, I worried. I worried hard and I worried as efficiently as I could. Then it occurred to me: I was doing it like I had done it when I was nineteen. Maybe when you don't practice for fifteen years, you miss the evolution of the blow job. Maybe as you mature together, your muscles relax or attenuate or adapt to the aging of your partner's member. Or maybe forty-year-old women who have been giving blow jobs for fifteen years are supposed to be giving blow jobs to men who have been receiving them for fifteen years. My imbalance blew his brains out.

He did not return from the shower. I went in after twenty minutes and found him slumped on the floor. Fortunately, when I smacked his face, he reacted, and his eyeballs still moved when I lifted his eyelid. I turned off the water and thought about what to do next. I didn't want anyone to walk into the bathroom and find Bruce passed out, naked and air-drying in the shower, and I didn't want to lock the bathroom door from the inside. I placed towels over his private parts and over his chest and roused the hostess, who turned out to be a retired nurse from Canada. She waved me towards the phone as she applied her stethoscope to his hairy breast. I heard her say, "Mr. Cavanaugh, breathe in deep. That's a good fellow."

I called the hospital and explained the situation, in as little detail as I could get away with. They sent an ambulance and I stayed with him at the hospital until seven the next morning. I wrote my own name in under next-of-kin. They did some extra tests and gave him some nutrition and exercise counseling, just to be on the safe side. They gave me a receipt and a packet of brochures about dieting, cholesterol, reasons to avoid strenuous exercise, and sexual responsibility. I stuffed them into my purse, waited for the twenty-something candy striper to maneuver a wheelchair full of Bruce's bulk into the lobby, called the Canadian nurse and asked her to charge the room to my credit card, and took him home.

❖

After such a terrible experience, I didn't really think things could go from bad to worse, but in the kismet of parenting, anything is possible, and usually probable. Bruce's faith that things would be handled fine by Julian during his brief but sole responsibility of the house could only turn out as erroneous as his faith that our trip would be romantic, sexy and relaxing.

I called Julian first, to let him know that Bruce had been in the hospital and that we were coming home. Julian's voice was tired but sweet and he expressed a great deal of concern for Bruce's welfare. I asked if anything went wrong last night and he said, no, he'd just hung out with some friends, ordered some pizza, watched movies. No problem. Julian was fourteen and I sort of trusted him. Mostly. Enough to call first when coming home, to give him a fighting chance.

Bruce was going to need someone to stay with him for about a week. I suggested his ex-wife, who was still a nurse. He glared at me. He asked if maybe we could get his mother to come, but his mother had broken her hip last year and would be of little help caring for Bruce. When he suggested my mother, I nearly pulled into the divider with shock.

My mother entered talking.

"So how's work?"

"Fine, Ma."

"You never see Zeke anymore."

"Ma, don't you remember what happened last time I went there?"

"Oh, that. That won't happen every time you go."

"I don't want to encourage it."

"Maybe you could put on some different makeup and he won't recognize you."

"Well, what would be the point of even going then?"

"Jesus would know that you'd gone to see your autistic brother."

"Do you really think Jesus would sit there smiling, holding Zeke's hand while he stroked off?"

"All I'm saying is that you don't make enough of an effort."

"George doesn't make an effort. At least I didn't expatriate!"

"We're not talking about George." Mom's lips pursed. "Zeke's sick," she said.

"What kind of sick?"

"He's got leukemia. The doctors say he's going to die within a couple months."

"Oh my God." My little brother was really ill.

"George called me a week ago and I told him, too. But he won't come home."

Fucker, I thought. God damn it! My little brother. Zeke.

"Where's my grandson? I love to see my grandson. There he is! Look at that height—just like George. But darker. Your father was some kind of Arab. But otherwise, you look just like your grandfather and your uncle. Maybe you'll get to see him someday, your uncle that is. Does your mother ever speak of George or does she pretend not to have a family anymore."

As I felt the slice of the backhanded commentary, Julian seemed surprised and happy to see his grandmother. She took his hand and started asking him about girls and school. I inspected for signs of partying that might remain from the night before. I sent my mother upstairs to turn down the sheets and ready our bedroom for Bruce.

"So Ma...what happened to him?" Julian asked me, as we helped him stand, ready to move him to our bedroom.

"I'm too fat," said Bruce.

"He passed out in the shower," I said.

"Were you in the shower with him?"

I glared at Julian.

"Okay. But you found him there? God, how gross!"

"He had an aneurysm. Basically, an artery in his head was blocked. That's called an embolism. Then it bursts. That's an aneurysm."

"So how did it burst?"

"I'm too fat," reiterated Bruce.

"I don't know? How do people get heart attacks? Or myocardial infarctions? Or strokes?" I asked.

"He had a stroke?"

"No, he…" My mother let out a horrifying scream, the kind that I had never imagined coming from so small a woman. Even when she'd walked in on my brother shooting a line of heroin into his Vietnamese wife's arm she'd never been this loud. I turned Bruce around so he could sit on the stairs, and ran up as fast as I could. My mother was in the doorway of my room.

A girl was staring at us, emitting these little shrieks. She was naked except for a pair of black silk panties and she had a belly button ring with a chain through it that looped around her waist. Right above her left breast was a tattoo of Casper the Friendly Ghost waving at her new audience. Her clothes, mostly leather and denim, were scattered around my bed, and a cat o'nine tails lay discarded on my rocking chair, the one where I'd nursed Julian. Both of her wrists were secured to my headboard by two pairs of my queen size control-top nude pantyhose. The lamp on my night table tumbled to the floor and somehow lit, though it did not break. She screamed and kicked at the corner of my 300-thread count down comforter which, like a last hope, slipped off the edge of the bed and disappeared off to the side. My underwear drawer was open and had been raided. My vibrator, like an obscene gesture lay naked on the floor.

My mother began to hyperventilate and I moved around her, trying to eclipse her view. I closed the door to the shrieking girl. Julian was behind me now and he saw what I had seen. He looked at me as if I were responsible for this. He charged into the room to quiet the girl. Through the door I heard her screaming and kicking and him saying, "shhh, I'm not going to hurt you." As the door closed behind him, my mother straightened up. At the top of the stairs, she took my hand and said, "you do what you want in your house, but I'm telling you your brother is dying." Then she descended the staircase, patting Bruce on the head, and settled herself on the sofa in the living room. I heard her change the channel from ESPN to the Home Shopping Network.

Julian moved the girl to his own bedroom, while Bruce and I sat on the stairway.

"Whoa," said Bruce. It was all he could manage.

"Whoa, yourself," I said. I kissed him on the forehead and told him that this was all his fault. He laughed a little and we put our heads together. When the bedroom was ready, Julian and I continued moving Bruce upstairs. I considered asking Julian whether he changed the sheets, but I just didn't care anymore. Bruce fell asleep almost immediately.

I wandered down the stairway, vertiginous, stabilizing myself with the railing. By the time I got to the kitchen, I felt like I was just catching up with myself. I put my head down on the kitchen table and waited until I heard Julian usher the strange girl out the front door. Birds were screaming in the trees just behind the windows. Maybe it was all of them reuniting after the hard winter up north, but they were creating such a racket I couldn't think. I heard Julian enter the room and I opened my eyes. I could see his white socked feet through the glass of the table.

"Ma, I'm so sorry."

"Who is she?"

"I don't know. I don't remember."

"Did you have sex with that girl?" I looked up at him.

"No! No! I had a party and I had it all cleaned up but I guess I didn't check your room."

"She was tied to the bed. She was tied to MY bed, with MY stockings!"

"I know."

"What kind of sick friend of yours would do this?" I put my head back down.

"I don't know."

"Is she okay?"

"Yeah. She's fine. She's okay. She was just really wasted last night."

"We could be sued for this. Is she a minor?"

"No. Actually..." I waited and then raised my head again. "Actually, she's a senior at the high school. Someone paid her to be there, but she won't tell me who."

"Jesus Alfuckingmighty."

I put my head down again. "Do me a favor, please. Can you check every single room in this house? I don't think I could take any more of these kinds of surprises. Enough for one morning, don't you think?"

"I made coffee..." he said.

"Thank God." I lay there with my cheek on the cold glass of the table while he poured a mugful. He left the room and I listened to every single door open and close. I raised my head when he reentered the kitchen and timidly slid my pink silk underwear across the expanse. In a black felt tip marker read the blocked letter message: "HERE'S YOUR UNDERWEAR BACK!"

7. Waiting For the Miracle

I know what a miracle is. I don't think I've ever seen one, but I definitely know what one is. I've spent a lot of time in my life thinking upon that very subject. When Anna May first changed her name, I took very little notice of the word itself, thinking mainly of rainbows and God's love and the easy uses of the word. Once she was gone, I thought a lot more about ways to find her, and I got caught up in the word. I read old hagiographies, lives of the saints. What I learned was that a miracle is something that can often easily be faked. It's a requirement for canonization that you have to prove (or someone has to prove) that you have performed at least three miracles. And it's not all turning water into wine—some of it seems more, well, useless than that. Some saints were canonized on the basis that it was proven that they hadn't had a bowel movement in three years. Some saints just ate dirt and were canonized. These things were called miracles, but from my perspective, if you're going to call something a miracle, it better have a some purpose to it.

I feel her, still, like I feel the death of my father. I dream about her, randomly, but the face I picture is not hers. I know it's not hers, but my dream logic gives it a face of someone I'm dealing with now. She's combing my hair and singing some protest song by Donovan and I'm watching my hair get longer and straighter in the mirror. It's a soothing dream, but it usually only happens when otherwise within the dream, I'm in the middle of gunfire or something unsettling like that.

There was a retarded girl who used to play with me and my brother, George, sometimes when we were in Barnesville. Her father had been gone all her life and her mother would clip pictures out of the newspaper and tell her they were pictures of her dad. We hung around in her house once, listening to the Sgt. Peppers side B, as she pored over the album cover, pointing to different celebrities in the portrait, some even female, and telling us they were her father. In a ragged, yellowing photo album, she had pictures of John F. Kennedy, Nikoli Lenin, Bob Dylan, Castro, J. Edgar Hoover, Marlene Dietrich, Ava Gabor, Peter Sellers, G. Gordon Liddy, Bob Hope and Jerry Garcia without the beard. Every one of them was her father. Once George tried to explain that you can't have a female father so Ava and Marlene were obviously not in the running, but her mother held his hands under searing hot tap water until he admitted that they were ALL her father, independently and one.

George was extremely angry and cursed and screamed and wailed as we ran all the way home. He wouldn't tell our mother until the next day, hoping that his hands would be healed by then. I brought him bowls full of ice water into the morning, but his hands were chapped and dark red by first light. As far as I know, he did chores all day long, gritting his teeth against the biting strap of the horse reins, the pointy texture of the chicken feed and the splintery wood of all the corrals. I went back to the woman; I had to know what happened to make her do that to him. I was the smarter one and better equipped to keep quiet when I needed to. Even though I knew George would tell our mother by the time I was gone, I ran all the way there, a good two miles, and settled in without breakfast, waiting on their lawn until the little girl woke and ran out of the house to cover me in slobbery kisses and ask me to read her books.

The thing that he got wrong was that all the pictures were the same person as far as the little girl was concerned. It didn't matter whether they were male or female, because they were exactly the same person. It wasn't so much that they weren't her father, but his saying so was blasphemy. Her mother explained it to me as we ate cream cheese and jelly sandwiches while the little girl watched *Bonanza* reruns. She explained how the Trinity was three people: God, Jesus and the Holy Spirit.

"Now, the Holy Spirit is in every person, right? You know that from your catechism, right?"

I had no idea what a catechism was, but I pictured George's bright red hands that split in long maroon ridges into the palms and I nodded.

"So," she continued, satisfied, "the Holy Spirit is in every person, right? And it is in every good, innocent child. Carley is a blessed child. Do you know why I say that?"

I shook my head no. I really wanted to answer that it was maybe because she was retarded, but I couldn't shake the picture of George's hands. Zeke had a couple years to be born, and that's when I would get my training about blessed children.

Her mother touched a space on the green quilted tablecloth in front of me, as if indicating the seat of the answer. "You should know; you're a smart girl. She's simple. She hasn't got anything to worry her head about. She just believes anything you tell her. Are you like that?"

"No, ma'am," I said, and took another bite of the cream cheese sandwich.

"But you know that I'm telling you the truth, right?"

"Yes, ma'am," I said, through a mouthful of masticated sandwich. I drank some apple juice to help me swallow faster.

"Don't eat so fast. Just nod yes if you want to say yes. I know you're a very smart girl, but that's why you have to watch out for devils. I keep the devils away from Carley, but you have to make your own decisions and you're going to have to pray for yourself." She stood and the girth of her hips reminded me of the backside of a horse.

"Yes, ma'am," I said. She poured me more apple juice.

"Your brother is the devil," she said to me, leveling her eyes as she placed the pitcher back on the pea-green counter. The ice cubes bobbing in the juice rattled against the plastic.

"I know, ma'am," I said. And I did know. Or I thought I did. Yesterday had been one of George's most mild transgressions; I knew him to be an unholy terror to me and to Anna May. But I still hadn't understood why all the people were her father, so I asked.

"You haven't figured that out yet?" she hooted. "If the Holy Spirit is in every person, then every person is the Holy Spirit and God and Jesus Christ." She narrowed her eyes. "Good people, that is…" She folded a brown rag and wiped the crumbs off the plastic tablecloth that hooked with elastic around the edges of the table. "So every person in the world, every good person, has a part of God in them. In that same way, they have Carley's daddy in them."

"Even me?" I asked, sure that I could not possibly have her father in me. Anna May had told me how babies are born and she said I wasn't old enough to be anyone's mother. Also, though I wasn't going to bring it up again, I knew that I could in no possible way carry anyone's father. The idea of one person as three people didn't confuse me as much as the idea of souls being the same yet separate. People looked similar to me, but I was constantly being surprised by the way people thought. And I still am.

"Some day. We'll see," she sang. Then she ushered me outside to watch Carley stuff her mouth with wet sand and smile, the grit stuck in her gums and between her teeth. I remember ruminating on all this new information, seeing, for a while, a spirit in everyone. Or what I thought was a spirit. I was looking for something similar but overt in every human being.

Years ago, when I was looking for Anna May, I read an article about a scientist who had attempted to quantify the soul. I'm sure many scientists time and again have worked to this end. He did actually come up with a tangible result: apparently, he placed eight subjects (at separate times, of course) who were extremely close to death upon a scale and waited until they passed. It wasn't quite as cruel as it sounds, as a measurement with pillows and blankets was allowed—but no family member, though present, could touch the body as it passed. He measured that the body prior to death was one seventy-fourth of an ounce, on average, heavier than the weight when it just passed. His findings were riddled with the testimony of aura-readers and purported clairvoyants and other dubious sources, so it didn't really convince me that the soul is something that inhabits a body and then is gone. However, I was thinking of this silly woman with her Off-Track Betting wall clock and her black velvet

Jesus wall hangings and filthy blessed daughter, and it made some amount of sense to me.

At any rate, I ran all the way there and ran all the way back, nearly puking up the cream cheese sandwiches that tasted like clabber milk and malt rye on the way back up. My mother was ready for me and I got a week's punishment for having known better. And I did. I thought I knew better than everyone.

❖

Girls in my family never blossomed into beautiful women like they say girls are supposed to. We kind of pro-wrestled attractiveness and it gave over in the end. Anna May was not naturally ugly like us, like the other women in our family, but she had those similar features. She had a beauty, like we all have a beauty. It's not natural beauty or internal beauty or any of that crap. Historically, we have painted, pruned, plucked, puckered, picked and poked until we are somewhat better looking than we started and then we muscle down the whole works. Our thighs are thick, faces broad, moles poorly situated and unapologetic, feet huge, breasts matronly and square, fingernails brittle and teeth widely gaped for luck. Our eyes have a depth that makes us look either easygoing or thickheaded, depending upon the viewer, and down to the very laziest one of the genetic line, we have remarkable natural strength.

But men found Anna May beautiful because she was confident. She had long beautiful strong legs (not without our thick thighs) but with tanning oil that was eight dollars a bottle back in 1965 shipped from France, she had contestably the best legs in Ohio. People forgave her crooked nose for her smile and reevaluated that dopey look we've all inherited to be lackadaisical wisdom. She wore lamé and gold foil and yet people forgave her eccentricities for her plump promising breasts and they giggled at her dye jobs and boy cuts until she ordered her new style and it became *de rigeur*.

I found some pictures of Anna May before she left—my mother had kept some of these eight-by-ten photos that she had done. They don't represent her at all, really, though they are obviously her. She had long hair in thin, broad, gold curtains and the photographer had obviously photographically capped her teeth. In some of them she was smiling and in some of them she looked horrified. Her hand partially eclipsed her wetly parted lips and her eyes were wide with surprise. She had had these done because she wanted to star in a horror film and apparently she was headed to the casting call the day she left us. She never made it there, or if she did, she didn't use her real or stage name, or she was so bad that they lost all her materials. Either way, there was no trace of her when we searched.

I still have the pictures. I found Julian cutting them up one day for a social studies project, so some of them have wedge shaped flaps peeling the grayish satin background away from her face, and some are just the circle of her face and the frame of her hair cut in short runs of flat lines where his young hands couldn't manage the scissors as well as we both might have liked. Some are still intact, though.

Julian's assignment was to do a family tree and he knew that these were pictures of his aunt. He drew very realistic likenesses of me, my mother and my grandmother, and all the rest of the spaces on the limbs were empty.

I started to write in what I knew, from what I was told by my mother. To my surprise, it was very little. When Anna and I would play, we would sometimes make up extremely long and involved relationships. We convinced a friend of Anna's that Paul McCartney was our uncle on my father's side. That Christmas, it had gotten all around Anna's school and tons of her friends showed up on our meager little farm to catch a glimpse of the superstar coming to visit his brother, but they were just chased away by my father in his old red pickup. We found ourselves related to Catherine Deneuve and Ernest Hemingway, Liberace and Janis Joplin. We could find resemblances between anyone we could think of. Anna told her friends how we were even related to the woman on the Aunt Jemima bottle. Our family was whatever we made it.

I looked at the blank spaces on the page and filled in what names I knew. Irene was married to George on my mother's side, and she was their only daughter. My father, Nathaniel Harvey, left his parents in Oklahoma where they died before I was born. After that I drew out four sticks, one for me, one for Anna, one for Zeke and one for George. Then I drew a line coming right out of me into a bubble containing Julian's name in all caps. The whole other side of the diagram was bare.

"Where do I put Bruce?" he asked.

I pointed to the paternal side.

"So where do I write in Abraham."

I waited for a moment, trying to decide between these men who was more important. Of course, it would have to be Bruce, but then this is a real family tree.

"Why don't we start again with this thing. I'm sure we can take some liberties…"

We drew another tree and we made space for everyone we knew about. Bruce and his mother, who we saw on most Christmases, fit in and Abraham and his wife. We even fit our cat in somewhere, and why not? Julian smiled at me when we were done.

"You know, Ma? That was pretty cool. I hate when they give you things and you have to do them their way."

That was in the glory days of mine and Julian's relationship. Before he became a monster and I was forced into being his mother, repeatedly.

Not that I minded and not that it would have made much of a difference to me, but he started to believe that he was African. He was Middle Eastern; I could give him that. He started to tell me, no matter what he did, that I wouldn't understand and that he believed that he was a reincarnated slave. He listened to Motown constantly, and rap. Again, not that I minded. I like some rap music, but he would play the same songs over and over and eyeball me like I was keeping him down. He grew out of that in about six months, when he decided that jazz was the best music in the world. Unfortunately this came slightly before Christmas, so I had to return all the selections from the Hip-Hop section that the cute cashier with a nose ring had patiently guided me through and walk with the tall gangly fellow whose glasses seemed to constantly slip off his nose. He handed me Bill Evans and Charlie Parker. Obvious names. George liked that music. He gave me Count Basie, which I definitely remember as my father's music. I handed that back. The biggest hit with Julian that year was a box set of Billie Holliday and a biography on her life. He would greet me or Bruce in the living room with a fact a day, but I was truly exhausted with the tinny sound of her voice emanating from the closed door to Julian's room. It was irritating, if only because I couldn't hear it properly. I laid down the law.

"If you are going to play nothing but that Billie Holliday album, I insist that you play it at full volume."

Bad idea. He turned it up up up so much that I couldn't hear anything above it. It was a constant battle. Fortunately, that lasted only a week.

Then he decided to go out for the wrestling team. I thought this would be a pretty innocuous sport, considering how brutal football is. (I was secretly glad he was never interested in baseball because it bored me to death.) He was running three miles a day and then going to practice, and meets were on Wednesday nights and Saturdays. He lost weight and gained weight and lost and gained. I was worried that the kid would be a huge stack of stretch marks come the end of the season. The worst was when I found him in his bedroom mummified in saran wrap to accelerate the fat shedding process. I was more than happy when, even though he did well for his weight class (one-twenty-three; he should have been at least one-sixty for his height), he decided against competing his senior year.

Then came his gothic phase. He wore all black and used my eyeliner and wore maroon lipstick. He stopped cutting his fingernails and for a while they demurely clacked against his glass at the dinner table and the remote control when he changed channels. When they grew out about an inch, they started to yellow and curl and simple chores became a problem. Bruce shook his head at me for allowing it and started carrying his football around the house wherever he went. All of the music emanating from Julian's room seemed to be sung by tenors approximating basses. The music was just as loud as the jazz he had played, and he painted over the peacock blue of the walls in his room with black. Then he used white and red paint to scatter tattoos and small murals whenever the spirit moved him. The spirit moved him more often to draw skeletons and vampyric faces than to do his trigonometry homework.

One evening I fell asleep very early in front of the television. I woke at about one in the morning and went to see if Julian was home. The car was idling in the driveway. I saw the shadow of Julian's profile through the blur of steam on the windshield. He seemed to be with a girl named Chaney from his school. She was a very prim, pink girl with two adorable splotches of reddened skin on the flats of her cheeks and a predilection for chocolate in any incarnation. Her soft pink shoulders and the doughy swell of the flesh below her collarbones were framed by an elastic furry brown tank top. They kissed and my heart flipped over. I know I was thinking that this was Julian's first kiss and I was so happy for him. Then they really started kissing. I closed the curtain and realized that he had been kissing girls for some time and not telling me about it. I never told my mother about kissing boys, not that there was much to tell, but what else could I expect? I couldn't resist and I looked out again. They seemed to be fully clothed, but I couldn't imagine that they would do something as stupid as have sex right in my driveway. They kissed like that for a quarter of an hour, during which time I made myself some tea. I tried to read a magazine article, but I couldn't concentrate on it knowing that they were so close. I watched a rerun of a sitcom that was on, and still Julian did not come inside. Like the mother I was at Disneyworld, I interfered. I turned on the porch light to signal that they should finish up. Nothing happened. I peeked through the curtains again and saw that they were still kissing. I walked outside into the cold. I was shivering as I approached the car, kicking gravel noisily, aiming for the tires. Still they kissed. I tapped on the window and they did not stop kissing. Julian had his hands around Chaney's cherubic face, but her eyes fluttered wide open and the irises rolled backward so that there was more white than color in the orbs. I backed away from the car, terrified, and emitted a little yelp as I tripped over a kid's bicycle that had been hidden by the dark. It must have been left by the I Want boys who apparently decided they no longer wanted. When I fell, I twisted my hip and the pain was excruciating, not to mention that the gravel had cut into my palm. Slanky had been crouched at the base of my rhododendrons and now we were on equal eye level. I looked back at the car and both Julian's and Chaney's faces stared out the window, their jaws both slightly agape, sizing up the situation. I lifted myself to my elbows and rested for a bit. Julian opened his door and said, "Whoa. Are you okay?"

"What are you doing?" I asked.

He started giggling as he helped me up.

"Are you stoned?" I asked.

"No. We're not stoned," piped Chaney in her cute little munchkin voice.

"Then what are you doing?" I noticed that neither one of them was wearing a jacket, yet Julian's head was soaked with sweat.

"Nothing. It's not a school night," he defended. The porch light was still on but distantly. Julian blinked rapidly. I looked at Chaney, who looked happier, friendlier.

"Why don't we go inside?"

"Chaney has to go home, but…" Julian began.

"What?" I asked.

"I can't drive. I mean, I shouldn't drive. I'm not stoned, but I shouldn't drive. Just trust me."

"Do you want me to drive you guys?"

"Mom?" Julian asked, "do we look okay to you?"

"What do you mean 'okay'?"

"I mean, normal. Not sick. Fine."

I stepped over to Chaney. I put my hand on her forehead and she closed her eyes and smiled. She was sweating too. When she opened her eyes, I saw the black pupils had nearly overtaken her irises. I wouldn't have been able to detect this symptom on Julian, as his irises, like his father's, were nearly black.

"Oh," I said. "What is it?"

"You won't get mad?" asked Julian. When I paused he said, "Promise you won't get mad."

"We'll see."

Julian looked at Chaney and she shrugged.

"It's ecstasy. It's a drug. It's not bad for you. Not like cocaine." Chaney's pager went off. "It's my parents. Can I stay here?"

"Call them first. Then yes. How tired are you two? Can you sleep? What do you need?" I asked. I'd had to talk Anna May down from a bad acid trip once. I had some experience, and I knew that regardless of what happened, now was not the time to disapprove. That would come tomorrow morning, or afternoon, depending on how long it took us all to fall asleep. They seemed concerned and alert, but content. I told them to walk around or dance or just keep moving until they felt better, and then to sleep. I ushered them inside and made up a bed for them in the basement. I suggested that Julian should spend the night in his own bed if he knew what was good for him, but that they could stay up for as long as they needed to.

❖

The next morning, my mother called to tell me that Zeke had died two nights ago. She was crying and I talked to her for a while on the phone. There was a lot of space between us, her sobbing and my silence, waiting for her to recover. It was probably unfair of me. But I didn't understand. I think when I left, I had given up on Zeke. I couldn't be in the same room with him for any amount of time. It was like having a gorilla for your brother. He never liked me and he was embarrassing. But he was my baby brother. That, I had to face.

My hip had a large yellow stain the color of bruised banana flesh and my neck was crooked in pain from sleeping on the couch and then talking to my mother on the phone. I drove Chaney home (she hugged me when getting out of the car) and returned to rouse Julian from the bed where he slept with Chaney, against my advice. We sat at the dinner table, drinking coffee. He looked worse than I did; the bags beneath his eyes were a bluish-black. Then I realized that it was probably just eyeliner smeared from last night. I decided to put off the drug talk until after the funeral, although I did make it clear that just because he was up late did not excuse him from my admonition that he was doing something that was both illegal and bad for his body. It also did not excuse him from the funeral. "Besides," I said, "you love wearing black."

"Your brother just died. How can you be so callous?" he asked.

I rubbed the sleep from my eyes and yawned and when I opened them again, he was gone from the kitchen.

Julian and Bruce attended the funeral with me and my mother. The casket was closed and we were the only four people standing at the silent vigil in the chapel of the care center. Bruce had ordered flowers, but the batch from us was dwarfed by the huge casket cover of roses my mother had sent. George didn't come back for the actual burial, but he had sent a small but lush vase of red flowers. I suppose that he never really knew Zeke, which I considered sad, sadder than Zeke's death and sadder than George's absence. Bruce held my mother's arm when she faltered walking through the sunny graveyard. I don't think I had a sense of it. All these bodies lying around me and I didn't have a sense of it. I didn't feel it.

When I was twenty-three, I was driving down a highway in Kansas, thinking about nothing in particular, and all of a sudden, like a premonition, the concept of death hit me. I was scared, since I was driving, and I realized that I didn't believe in God. I remember the war my brother went off to, and how he came back changed, crazed, an animal almost. He wasn't right. He snarled at us and he spat on the furniture. When he went back to Asia, we were all glad to see him go. The fear was that he would die, and when he didn't die, we realized what was worse, and what there can sometimes be in death.

Anna May didn't die either. She was eaten. She was just gone. We didn't have to mask over these tragedies with euphemisms. They were just gone. My father died in his sleep. He was a strong, generally quiet man, but he had two strokes before dying. I remember calling home from college during the days that I had no money. I sometimes turned off my phone service to cut down expenses. After not having spoken to them in a month, I called from a boy's house, the first night I ever had sex. I was sitting in the boy's living room, a crocheted blanket wrapped around my skinny body. My mother told me that my father had a stroke. The television was on in the stinky room, but the volume was all the way down and the news was showing clips of the baseball game from the night before. I watched the batter hit one out of the park, sailing over the fence. That's how I came to associate the word stroke, the thing that happened to my father, with the pop of a bat meeting a baseball, as if it were my father's head. He had another one, less eventful, and then he died in his sleep.

My mother told me after we cremated him that she always slept face up and she slept on his left side, one leg crooked over his thigh and her arm stretched across his chest. She said that when she was younger, she couldn't sleep unless he was snoring. It was his peace that brought her peace. She said that she woke up the minute his heart stopped beating. She said that he slept right through the moment of his death, but she woke, sensing the cessation of the blood through his chest and the quiet that followed so many years of snoring. She said she didn't sleep for two weeks except in spurts and only when the television was on. That's when she began working straight through the week and sleeping all weekend. She had plenty of money by the time my father died, but I think she was afraid that if she stopped to think, she'd die too.

Again, a presence sputtered before it died. And now Zeke, having sat in a care facility for twenty years. I could imagine his days: wake up and eat, run on the trampoline, eat, run on the trampoline, masturbate, sleep. It was what he did when he was at home. Maybe they had other activities, but I never asked. My brother was as good as dead. It seemed a shame, but not much more than a shame.

Julian asked me in the car on the way home, "So what happened to you when you were a kid? Why is our family like this?"

"Like what?" I asked, tugging innocently on the shoestring that held back the dam wall.

"Your sister ran away, your brother ran away, your other brother just died and you haven't cried once."

"I'm not sad," I said. I tried to find where the calm was in my head. "I think he suffered when he was alive."

"You don't know that."

"He had leukemia. That's a painful disease."

"Did you know that he asked for you? Grandma told me that. Did you know that when he died, he only weighed eighty-five pounds? Did you know that he once drank a whole bottle of shampoo because he was thirsty? I know more about your own brother than you do."

I was quiet. Then I said, "He asked for me?"

"He asked after me too, but you never cared to find that out. You never knew that. I think your sister left you on purpose. All of you are freaks, every one of you running away from what you don't understand. You don't want to believe that anyone really loves you because it'll hurt too much. Why don't you guys get married? Is it because you're waiting for something better to come along? I think you're too afraid to take a chance. I think you have problems in your head."

Bruce tapped the backs of his fingers against the inside of the window.

"When did you learn all this? On your vision quest last night?"

"As a matter of fact, yes. It became very clear to me. I understood a lot because of last night."

"So you do drugs and you become a PhD in Psychology?"

Bruce snorted. Julian stared into my rearview.

"You're just afraid that I've got you figured out. You think you're so smart and you can just hold everyone at an arm's length and judge them. But you need love so desperately. I've always known that. I don't need drugs to tell me that."

I learned to wait through his diatribes. I could put a thick layer between me and my son if I wanted to, like a layer of vacuous space. I could leave my body and just float, not worry about what he was saying. The first time he said, "I hate you," I learned how to do it, and I'd been perfecting the measure ever since. He was poking and scratching at the membrane, but it wasn't reaching me. Of course, that is until I realized that he was talking about the membrane. He was trying to reach me. He was coming too close.

"Look, honey. I told you before—I'm all you've got."

"I want more."

"I love you, Julian."

"'I love you, Julian,'" he mimicked me. I felt like there was all this space in the car, too much of the same old air moving around. I felt like I was slipping. I didn't feel well at all. I pulled the car over and ran to the grass beside the interstate, which looked greener than I can ever remember it. I saw the little heads of dandelions waving in unison with the sweep of every rushing car.

Julian had rolled down his window. "What are you doing?"

I looked at the sky. It looked too blue and too real.

"I," I began. And I stopped there and got back into the car. It didn't turn over the first time and sputtered angrily before easing into a second rev.

We rode.

After driving in silence for a little bit, I said, "I say the word 'I' too much."

We rode.

Finally, he said, "I'm sorry." So did I.

"I just want to know why it is that your family seems to be running away from each other every chance they get. Why doesn't anyone want to know about me?"

"I don't know, baby," I answered. "Sometimes that's the way people are."

"I can't accept that," said Julian. "I won't accept that."

"I love you," said Bruce. "I don't say it much, kid, but I love you both. And I choose to be with both of you, so don't pull any of that crap on me. I don't have to be here, but I want to. I want to know you and I want to love you."

I saw Julian nod and start biting the skin on the side of his thumb. After Bruce, who was never so demonstrative, came out with that, something inside me snapped. I was happy. I was truly, no holds barred, happy. I felt happy and very much loved and part of something free to whirl out of control at any second, but it was something real. It practically felt like a miracle.

❖

That night, in bed, after slow, quiet lovemaking, I slipped downstairs to make some cocoa. When I came back, the light was off.

"I'm turning on the light, okay honey?"

"No. No, don't." He shielded his eyes.

"Okay." I navigated in the dark to my side of the bed. "Were you just asleep?"

He was silent for a moment. Then he said, "I don't know."

"Are you okay?"

"I'm just thinking about death. It's getting me down, you know? I mean, we're getting old."

I was forty-three years old. I had Julian when I was twenty-six and I started graying the year after he was born. I held off the gray for a little while with some of that expensive Henna shampoo, but it was no use. There were more brown hairs turned gray every day I didn't use the shampoo than I could keep up with. I was old and fat and tired, so tired all the time. And he was only forty-six, but he was sedentary and worn down. He was never a sexy man, but he was gruff and solid like a bear when I met him. Now his cheeks drooped and his abdomen bloated in that puffy kind of box that happens to aging men. He was still tall and imposing, but the hair on his chest, arms and back had started to turn from red-blond to a lighter and downy silver. This was no overnight thing; it had been happening for years.

"Honey, we've been old. We're relics!" I said. "It's not our world anymore. Look at the number of double strollers and suburban sprawl and everything in the world. A generation of the baby boomers' children is moving in on us, dominating the market, defining the trends. We're dinosaurs. There's two of them for every one of us."

"Why do you say that? I don't want to be old."

It was true. For the last two Christmases I had bought Nerf guns and footballs for my boyfriend and ties for my son. The world was turning upside down. I shrugged and climbed into the bed with him.

He said, "You know, I spent a lot of time in my life trying to figure out what was the point. When I was younger, death always seemed so close. I felt like I just had it coming, like I was daring it to walk in and take me. There were times when I desperately wanted to die. I was never afraid of it. Now I'm fucking terrified. I suppose that it's when you're happy that you fear it the most. It's like you can only really see what you have with plenty of light."

I started to ask him to tell me a joke. Since our first day together, it was what made him happiest—getting me to laugh. He still sounded close to tears, though, unusual for him. And I figured now was a time to respect his seriousness. So I touched his shoulder, ran my fingernails through the short red stubble on the back of his neck, and listened. I'd heard parts of the story before, but not all of them, and certainly put together in context.

"I was really messed up for a while, like I told you. I was a true fuck up. The first two times I was in jail I thought of absolutely nothing except what I was going to do to get back to my drug-buddies as soon as I got out. It was my religion, as if it were a clean, good thing. A quest. You have a lot of time to yourself with your own thoughts when you're in jail, and I kept it simple. Get back to coke. Don't be stupid. Don't get caught. An easy goal.

"There were two regular guys I could buy from. The first guy was usually better because he had better stuff. A better supplier. His apartment was in an old fancy building on Fifty-Seventh street in the city, New York. You wouldn't have ever thought that this place was a drug den; it was more like a museum or a culture palace. He had pictures by famous artists and it made you feel rich and famous just going there. He even had a butler. This guy had power and class, but you could tell that he was not too removed from the street. He had Italian shoes and Italian suits and English shirts. My guess is that if you really knew about fashion, you'd get your shirts from a place even farther removed, so that you were really cutting edge, ahead of the times. Also the pictures that he had up were beautiful, but they looked old, like they were copies of real ones somewhere. You go into one of those SoHo galleries and they don't use those big gold frames anymore and the paintings are always pictures of things, not just portraits. All the ones he had on his walls looked like they were from the Seventeenth-century France. I don't know.

It just made him look less than one hundred percent, you know what I mean?"

I nodded.

"But if there was anything that he did know about absolutely without any question, it was food. He had training videotapes of great chefs running all day long in his living room. Apparently he had been a head chef at *Chez Paul* on 55th until his cocaine habit got in the way.

"He told the story like this: he wanted to do a line in the bathroom to get him through the next couple hours, so he took his Sabatier five-inch knife and a slip of paper to roll and snort with into the bathroom. Just as he chopped up a line, one of his sous-chefs set an arm on fire with one of the flambés. My drug dealer, the chef, rushed out of the bathroom and helped put out the fire. When he went back to the bathroom, he saw that the coke was gone. One of the busboys said that he saw it out in the open and put it into a plastic baggie before anyone noticed.

"It wasn't a big deal that he did coke or anything. Most guys running restaurants do something in order to keep going. The real shit hit the fan because in order to tell confectioner's sugar from flour, the pastry chef always left a slip of white paper in the bag or box or whatever so that he didn't have to taste it. So he, thinking that this little baggie was extra confectioner's sugar, dusted it across a tray of tartlettes. It was served before my guy figured out what happened. People complained of dizziness and vomiting and whatnot and my friend was fired the next day.

"He gave up coke altogether, but his reputation was ruined. It was either work short order or proofread menus or, in order to maintain his standard of living, buy and sell cocaine. But in that apartment, oh, could you eat! Duck steak with walnut raspberry sauce, chilled Asian pear soup, black bass ceviche with spearmint, Dover sole, oxtail consommé. I ate like a king. I picked up some French cooking tips, too. And I'm the only construction worker I know who can tell the difference between sevruga and beluga caviars."

I smiled. That's how I got fat, too, I guessed. French cooking New York style. It was just a matter of time.

"Anyway, the rules were that you did not come there lit and you did not get lit while you were there. If you were high on coke you wouldn't be hungry and that was just wrong, according to this guy. Or if you were baked, aside from smelling like weed and the chances being that you were unreliable and undesirable anyway, you wouldn't appreciate the delicacy of the food. And if you were a junkie or a dusthead you came nowhere near my buddy's place because his butler would kick your head in and toss your body out the back window, and no one would ever notice.

"There were beautiful women and there were beautiful men if that's what you were into, but most of them were paying off debts. I'm not a beautiful man, so when it got to be too much for my tab to handle, he would have me do other things, like beat up people who owed him. Or worse. I was always an asset because of my strength.

"But sometimes when I needed to cool it from this guy, I would head over to Jersey City because there was a guy there who would sell for way less, but his stuff was often cut with dust or cyanide. You couldn't ever tell until someone ODed. It was a true crack den type place—the kind you read about. You got to it by using a wooden ladder that you leaned against the metal frame of the fire escape, and let me tell you, every step felt like my last. The whole thing was this rusted, greasy metal screeching against metal, and the courtyard was paved with bricks, the only padding was broken flowerpots, cigarette butts, trash and hobo shit. It stunk of stagnant water and urine. Then you climbed to the third floor and swung a two feet expanse to the window ledge into the window, which, if he knew you were coming, he left open. Sometimes you had to knock and that was a bitch because he might not be home or he might be incapacitated, you know? And there you were, swinging, waiting, trying not to die."

Bruce opened the window to the roof of our house. We both climbed out so he could have a cigarette.

"You have to understand that we were three stories up and the swing over was not easy. You literally had to step over the railing, hold on with one hand and wrap your foot around the iron so that as you swung towards the ledge, if you fell, you could pull yourself back up. There wasn't anything on the ledge itself to hold onto, but about an inch of window sill that you could plant your toes on if the window wasn't open. There was a girl who tried climbing up with me once. Her name was Mona. She went first and she caught her high heel around the railing and almost fell, but I caught her. She was so strung out she kept saying, 'let me die, let me die,' but you can't believe a person like that. They don't know what they want.

"And once you were inside, it smelled like being back in jail. There was this sort of interstitial space that you swung into. There was a long brick hallway that not only did I have to hold my breath to go through, but I had to duck. They called it the birth canal. Then you got to this guy's place which was literally disgusting. The kitchen sink was stacked with pots, each of which had one spoon stuck to the bottom of it. They never got cleaned. The toilet never worked so the bathroom sink and kitchen sinks had piss stains in them. And the degenerates who hung around this hellhole smelled worse than I'm sure lepers do and puked where they slept...whatever. It was disgusting. And also, this guy sold everything you could think of and at all different prices, so it was pretty dicey. He took anything, food stamps, stolen credit cards, green cards, passports."

I briefly thought about Bruce's passport.

"So I was just out of jail for the third time and I was driving to the Fifty-Seventh street place. I wore a new tie, because I wanted to look respectable. You didn't call these guys first; it just wasn't done.

"It was cloudy that day and I was thinking about God. I was, kind of praying, you know. I was thinking that if God could just let me get high once more, I promised I would never do it again. I had truly had enough of jail. I don't even want to talk about that. But I needed it, just to forget for one last time and then I would face the world knowing what I'd been through. I'd be a survivor. But I couldn't survive without falling one last time.

"The Fifty-Seventh street place had been sold. The new owner said that he only heard, second-hand, that the guy who owned the place had died of a heart attack. Nothing more; just a simple heart attack.

"I remember the guy because he was a distinguished looking black man. The whole place smelled like incense or patchouli and all the art had been replaced with African tribal masks. I remember thinking to myself, this isn't the place; this is not the same place. I was pissed off at this man who had colonized the apartment, but I got a little crazy. Okay, I got a lot crazy. First I asked, 'Look, could you help me out?'

"This guy who had just looked all sympathetic, thinking that I was probably an estranged family member or something, steeled up. He said, 'I'm sure I have no idea what you mean.'

"'Look, speed, coke, meth. I'll take prescription shit, anything,' I pleaded. I eased my foot into the doorjamb so when he slammed the door he wouldn't be able to shut it all the way.

"He said, sweetly, through his smiling teeth, 'Will you take your junkie ass out of my apartment before I call the police?'

"I grabbed him. His wife or girlfriend or whoever, a thin white woman with a blood colored towel on her head came out of the bathroom, right at the end of the hallway, in a big pile of steam. Then she screamed and jumped back into the bathroom, and for some reason, the guy lunged at me. I left running. I remember thinking that everything and nothing was going on in my head. No specifics, just everything and nothing, everything and nothing. I felt like I understood it for the first time, how everything and nothing could be simultaneously upon you, working you. I had no sense of who I was or what I was doing. It was a fat stream of loose sense coming at me as I drove. Maybe the black guy killed the old chef. Maybe I had the wrong door. Maybe he was lying. Maybe he hated me. Maybe God hated me. Maybe I wasn't even here.

"I lit out of there as fast as I could, heading for Jersey City. I drove my mother's car through the Holland Tunnel and found that the second guy's entire building had been destroyed. There was a new building with no sign of the place that had been there before. The back stairwell had been renovated and you couldn't reach the fire escape any more. I felt the same way, like things had just been replaced, shifted around. The world was not the same world I left. I had only been in jail seven months, but I didn't expect everything to change so fast.

"I was crazy. I went back to the car and just drove and drove. It was about three o'clock in the afternoon and I was out of my mind. I looked at the impenetrable clouds through the filthy, bug-spattered windshield and I said out loud that if God wanted me to never take another drug in my life he should show me a sign. Like a fucking miracle, the sun broke through the clouds. I didn't want to admit it, so I dared Him to show me another. The clouds covered the sun and then broke through again. So I laughed. I laughed and laughed as I drove. I waited until the sun had moved behind this big motherfucker of a cloud, a real monster, and I said, 'break through that you son of a bitch,' and it did. It did."

Bruce smiled and chuckled. I laughed a bit too, trying to picture it.

"But then, it got really good. I said, just as I was heading into the Holland Tunnel, out loud, in the car, 'I don't believe you.' I said, 'I can't. I won't. I can't.' Maybe I thought I could get away from Him if I was in a tunnel, unable to see the lightshow in the sky. I don't know—if there was a point where I was just desperate for something, anything at all, it was then. And, of course, that's when it happened. Believe it or not, in the middle of the left lane, about a quarter mile in, was a woman lying on the ground, recently hit by a car that hadn't stuck around. I stopped my mother's car, leaving it running with the parking brake on and went to the woman. She was breathing. She looked like she'd been hit on the side. Her hip was bruised and swollen through a tear in her jeans, and she was bleeding from her eye, her lip, her chin and the top of her head. Her wrist was bent back, her knuckles bent back against her forearm. She was calling out something in Spanish and she had blood all down the right side of her body. I held her down, trying not to let her move her head. I was wrecked by this, but I went into a sort of emergency mode and started yelling at all the people (and a good number had gathered at about this point) to call an ambulance and set flares and everything. All of a sudden, all these people and I were working like a team. There was some guy who set himself to the task of redirecting traffic and some woman was talking on her cell phone and while I held this poor lady's hand and tried to talk to her in my simple pidgin Spanish a nurse was taking her pulse and wrapping cloth from a first aid kit around her wounds. It was amazing. I thought, 'okay, you win, you fucker.'"

He smiled at me. I smiled back at him.

"That's not much of a miracle," I said, "or 'sign from God.'"

"It's just that I knew it was. It could have just been a, I don't know, a newspaper or something in the street, which is definitely not a miracle, but if I felt it, it would have been."

"I guess that's why so many people *do* believe in God. At some point, you really get a dose of belief."

"I don't know about everybody," he said.

"Not me, yet," I said.

"Nope, not you yet." He leaned back and closed his eyes. Smoke curled from our cigarette which rested between his third and fourth fingers of his right hand.

"It hit me right then how precarious it all is."

"What?" I asked.

"Life. Everything. Nothing. I could have been anything in life. A cricket or a spider or anything, but I'm a human being. And there is a God somewhere out there who is telling me stuff all the time, if I only take the time to listen. I had the capacity to help this girl even though I spent so much time trying to get stuff that I thought I needed. It was a sign that my body could have been just as easily destroyed, falling down the back of a crack den fire escape, dying of a heart attack, being hit by a car at any point when I was crossing the street."

"You believe that?" I asked.

"Heart and soul," he said. "With everything I've got. It was a true bitch keeping clean. It still is."

"Did the woman live?" I asked.

"Yes, indeed," he said, his answer windy with breath. He rubbed the faces of his thighs. "I married her. And then she divorced me."

"Oh. That was Elena."

"They do say that God giveth and He taketh away. I suppose I learned my lesson."

I listened to the population of crickets in Folsom emanate their nightly songs from the distant reeds and shrubs and bushes. All those souls who could have so easily been human. I thought about nucleic acids, how all organic matter is the same stuff at the molecular level, just phrased differently, said in a different way.

"We're not so old," I said and laughed. "We're just weighted down with experience."

"Thank you for saying that, Karen," he said.

"Anytime."

PART III
THE BIG QUEEN

8. Lovers

I'm sure part of the reason that I'd never considered marriage before now is that I've already married my cat. I married the house cat, named Leonardo, when I was eight years old, under my parents' coffee table in our living room. I remember lighting a ceremonial candle in the dark, rain streaming down the windows, and a black smudge of spent sulfur on my thumb as I tried to keep Leonardo purring. I was deeply in love with the cat and sure that he returned all my affections. I wore my mother's long white apron on my head, carefully angled so the blue lace pocket didn't show, the waist strings tied thickly below my long brown hair. I mumbled the vows so that no one could hear me be so stupid and ridiculous and I looked deeply into Leonardo's eyes to find acquiescence to the vows, if not concord. I'm sure he looked at me long enough and seriously enough while one of my hands held his head and the other stroked the fear out of his back, that I assumed he understood his role in our marriage. It wasn't much—I just wanted someone to understand me and love me, and come when I called.

I walked around like a married woman, or what I thought a married woman would look like: self-satisfied, happy, in charge. I tied a string around my wedding ring finger when no one was around. I kept it tucked in the top pocket of my overalls when I wasn't wearing it. I lost it at some point in the laundry.

Leonardo died when I was twelve, so I suppose I'm a widow. But the four years that we were married, I always expected to be stricken down by God for blaspheming a rite of the Lord. My reasoning vacillated between thinking that He was not going to punish me because I was young and *suffer all the little children* and all that, and thinking that He was punishing me by making me obsess about marriage when I was so young. I couldn't take it back, and I didn't want to. I wanted that cat to be my husband—my mother had a husband and he took care of her, in a way, and lived with her weird motivations and quirks without complaint. I wanted someone to know me that well, and I guess I believed it was going to be my cat.

I'd forgotten about the solemnity with which I entered the contract by the time I was nine. I didn't care much for boys, so I hadn't narrowed the playing field to exclude feline and other non-human species or anything. I think my cat must have let me down—not come when I called or something. I was aware that children were allowed much that could be attributed to whim, so I didn't beat myself up for forgetting. In fact I think I was much relieved when I realized that I'd forgotten the vows. And so many things occurred to me later that I wouldn't have thought of when I married him, like how I would kiss him or how we would make a living. I'm sure I would have spent a lot of time laughing at myself if I hadn't maintained a pretty solid horror at my own heresy.

After my first lover, Leonardo, homo sapiens didn't look so great. The thing I couldn't get used was the talking, all the communication and sharing feelings. I'm glad Julian came into my life to teach me about that stuff because I couldn't sit still to listen to anyone before I had to force myself to pay attention to that poor kid. But baggage is very real and I didn't want anyone walking into my heart and dumping a whole lot of stuff on me. I wanted a quiet, self-cleaning man who, when he wanted my attention, he would just crawl up on my book and rub his side in my face. You can see the problem in launching a search based upon these criteria.

The second person I loved was one of the forwards on our basketball team. Her name was Jennifer MacGregory and I wanted to be just like her. I remember running my ruined fingernail over her yearbook photo, her long, soft, curly hair falling across her shoulders as if it were recently unclasped from a barrette, and her eyes behind her small metal in-vogue glasses were bright with the light from the photographer's flash, but they were animated and friendly, as if she were amazed with the simplicity of something as usual as ants disappearing into their hill or a leaf blown in the wind. It was easy to believe I knew her; her face invited it. I watched her in school and sometimes she would pass an insider's smile my way, letting me in on the joke.

I took classes just to be near her. She was the kind of interesting intellectual girl who suffered from an absolute lack of common sense. She would achieve perfect scores on her tests but she would also ask the most sophomoric questions, questions that students like me were afraid to ask. She could memorize without application and I admired that. I wanted a simple life. I wanted to be her. Maybe, if I think about it, I wanted my sister back.

When Jennifer became pregnant, she became withdrawn and sullen. She refused to admit who the father was, though everybody except her parents knew that it was Sean McCarthage, a boy from one town over who had a great reputation within the CYO. Suddenly, pregnant, she became older and wiser than all the other girls who believed that they represented progress by wearing platform shoes instead of the regulated loafers, or who started fires on school grounds in protests of freedom or feminism or stopping the war. Her friends dropped away from her as her stomach grew. I thought it might be because she was freakish, like I was. But it was because she stood on a pedestal, she was untouchable. She was a martyr, someone that you didn't want to be like, the name mothers whispered to their daughters when they talked about sex. I was just different and ugly. No mother warned about my fate. No daughter cared about me.

I remember rehearsing what I was going to say to her in the hallway. I knew all her classes and when they met. I was going to cut her off at the door to the lunchroom and just follow her for a bit before she ducked into the girls' lavatory before eighth period. I thought that way if things went badly I could just cut out early and it wouldn't count against me.

My initial speeches sounded corny, contrived and completely unbelievable. I tried to imagine her listening to me babble on and almost talked myself out of talking to her. I wanted to ask her if she could teach me to play basketball. I pictured her looking down at her stomach and then at me and walking away in disbelief. Then I thought I would just tell her I loved her. She had to deal with that. She might say that she was pregnant and that I wouldn't want her, but of course, I knew about babies and I could raise babies. But the idea of her doing anything other than slapping me hard in the face made me feel queasy and raw inside. I honestly didn't know what I wanted from her.

So I came up with the idea of asking her to let me be there when she gave birth. I talked myself through it with the following logic: I thought that she might need someone there, since it was widely known that her parents were divorced. She lived with her father, an auto mechanic who threw wrenches at kids who came near his place, and he would never want to be there at the birth. But the clincher was this: I was going to tell her I was studying to be a midwife. I read a couple books on midwives and I was prepared to tell her exactly what they do in case she asked. So I did it: I walked up to her in the bathroom, expecting to tell her exactly what I had prepared.

That she had a cigarette in her hand was the first unexpected thing to happen. A thick chemically film of recently spritzed hair spray and the long ache of tobacco swirled in the air as I pushed open the lavatory door. Her face was that familiar one in the photograph, with a little too-white powder smudged over a nascent pimple on her jaw line. She was definitely showing, and she was at least five months along, though she wore her National Honor Society cardigan in order to conceal it. She looked embarrassed of her delinquent hand, uncasually, stiffly holding the cigarette. Then she regained her determination and said, "hey."

"Hey," I said, heading over to wash my hands. She had spoken out of turn. I pulled a towel from the dispenser and said, "When are you due?"

"What are you, a fucking narc?" she growled and took another nervous drag. I realized that she thought I was policing her tobacco use.

I don't know why I did it. I can't remember how it occurred to me and all I truly know is that I couldn't help it. I reached my hand out to her swelling belly and, surprisingly, she let it rest there. Her face flushed and she started to cry. I took the cigarette from her, leaving my other hand on her belly.

"I don't even smoke. I just bought them. I don't know," she started crying, her eyes turned up to the dropped ceiling tile. I followed her view. Several tampons that had been soaked and slapped up to the ceiling flagellated their strings to the beat of the overhead fan.

"I wanted to know," I began, my tongue feeling like an alien, "If you've considered having a midwife." I had a whole speech here, but I dropped it, "Because I'm one. I mean, I'm in training."

"You mean like a test tube baby?" she asked ingenuously. She wiped her tears. I let my hand drop.

"No, no. I mean like home birth. Not letting a doctor deliver it, but a midwife."

"Oh," she said, obviously unable to handle me right now, in her face, asking me procedural questions about her birth. "No. I have a doctor."

"Can I be there?" the words just marched out of my mouth, on their own, just the soldiers I had taught them to be.

"What?" she asked.

"I mean, as your midwife. But of course, you have a doctor. I mean, I don't know if you can have both. Midwifery is so natural."

The bell rang. We were both late.

"I don't think so," she said, but made no motion to leave.

I closed my eyes. "I love you," I said.

I didn't hear anything at all except her breathing. Then I heard a toilet flush. I opened my eyes and wondered if I had imagined it.

"I'm going to pretend that I didn't hear that," she said. "It's weird. You're weird. You have no idea who I am."

"You're so lucky," I said.

"I'm lucky? I'm lucky?" she asked. "This fat stomach is luck?"

"Your baby will love you. You will never be alone."

"I'm fat, I'm depressed, I'm off the team, I can't think straight, I'm hungry, I'm sweating all the time. I'm lucky. And I've got freaks coming up to me in the bathroom telling me that I'm lucky and that they love me."

"I'm sorry," I said.

A stall door swung open. A girl with thick looped braids whom neither of us recognized ran out of the bathroom with her hands over her ears. The door swung shut slowly. Smoke from the cigarette was still rising from the porcelain sink. When I looked to it, I noticed that there was a brown stain growing against the white of the bowl. How many times had I washed my hands wondering where such stains came from?

"Just leave me alone." She said, stepping past me. I longed so much to touch her stomach again. "Just remember that I'm what happens when you fuck up. I'm what happens when you think you love someone and you don't."

❖

There was no one but Anna May before that or after. I love my mother like you have to love a mother. You don't choose to love a mother. I had sex twice in college with two anonymous men with too much back hair and too little head hair, each time after a long night sitting alone at my favorite bar and each time with disaster striking in the morning. The first time, as my one-night stand lay naked on top of the sheets, his penis shriveled into a wet smirk, and in the background I heard the pop of a bat against a baseball, my mother told me that my father had had a stroke.

The second time when I woke up, the guy whose name I don't remember said, "Okay. It's time for you to go." I understood and dressed while he was in the bathroom emptying his bladder into the toilet while brushing his teeth. As I opened the door to leave, I heard him spit and flush. I returned to my tiny apartment to find it ransacked. The only things missing, the only things of value I had, were a well-hidden coffee can with my tutoring and job money kept in it, and my chemistry textbook. I remember that upon returning home I looked up to the cracked ceiling, focusing on not the floor above me that held a fat ex-cop who slowly, unfailingly, skipped rope for a half hour every midday, and not on the next floor up where my lazy old pattering landlord, whose feet never donned any shoe but slippers, and who had apparently not fixed the lock, lived. But I looked up to the blue sky outside, into the clouds where I imagined God was seated at a huge command center, pushing buttons and laughing heartily. I looked up to Him and his omnipotence for an answer for the way I was being treated, for the answer to the obvious question. Okay, okay, I get it. No premarital sex.

There was a news show on the television once about inner city women and their babies. I remember that there was one woman when asked why she decided to get pregnant, she said, "I just wanted someone to love me." I am capable of being that selfish. Julian's love seemed like everything to me for years, just like Abraham's love did for those two weeks. And I can't say that I did not have periods of loneliness I never thought would abate. Julian was my only happiness in those times. And I never thought that anyone could really choose to love me.

And so I wound up with Bruce. Bruce came into my life a neutered cat—simple and sexless, and he would even come when I called. After we started having sex and he started spending nights in my bedroom, (or I vacationed in the basement), nothing really changed. He changed some of the utilities, like the cable, to his name and I managed anything that had to do with the house. Other than that, all financial responsibility was mine and in my name. I took out an insurance policy, naming him as the beneficiary, but leaving a stipulation that Julian would get the money when he turned eighteen. This was the biggest step to commitment I made. Even after the vacations and the roses and the way he sometimes took me out to dinner, it was like playacting. I was pretending I was a beautiful lady and he was my gorgeous suitor. What I suppose we really looked like was local access' answer to *Roseanne*. I gained weight, no longer having to do the simple tasks like taking out the garbage, and he let his reddish hair eclipse the big pink stubbly cheeks, so he looked like a giant muppet. We weighed nearly five hundred pounds put together and with stringy Syrian Julian running around, I assume we were regarded as, if not abductors, adoptive parents.

Bruce came home one summer night very drunk. The car was parked askew on our lawn and he was laughing and giggling when he walked into the house. I was fuming and I shook his arms yelling that he should never drive drunk. He was laughing and he smelled like gin and sweat. He fell down to his knees and said, "You have to marry me. You have to marry me because I can't live without you." He was disgusting, his hairy filthy body reeking and his coordination gone. I had begun peeling his work shirt off his arm but I dropped him right there and went upstairs to lock myself in the bathroom. I expected him to come up, try to cajole me out of the room. I was prepared for the worst. But the worst was that he didn't do anything. I heard his hoary laughter for a while and then I heard it die out. I washed my face with cold water and kicked the bathroom scale deeper beneath the sink. I looked at my broad cheeks in the mirror, unwilling to accept the loss of the girl I once knew well sunken below the wrinkles and graying hair and the swell of my huge double-chin. I was disgusted daily by my own appearance. This was the only mirror I owned (though Julian had four in his room alone!) and I avoided it whenever possible.

I brushed my hair with my long neglected hairbrush. Static sparks flew from each combing line and the hair raised off my head. Long wiry broken wisps of gray lifted up into the atmosphere and the brown ones stayed put. I found some cold cream and put it on the circles under my eyes. Other than that, my medicine cabinet held nothing more than three bottles of antacids, some aspirin, alcohol and an antibacterial/antiburn agent. I had no cosmetics at all. I had some perfume that Julian gave me for a Christmas seven years ago and a crusty bottle of nail polish, nearly spent. I washed away the cold cream and used water to dampen the errant strands of gray. I listened for Bruce, or Julian and heard nothing.

The next morning, Bruce said nothing to me about the incident. He didn't ever ask me to marry him again. We just lived together, slowly going about our lives as if this was a perfectly normal way to go. My kid, my house, his understood presence. We had sex again that night. He told me a joke and I laughed and he kissed me. We lay pressed on the bed against each other trying to get every possible exposed part to feel the other one's body against it. His sweat rose like a film between us, but like a sucking film, a film meant to bind.

WHAT HAPPENED TO THE MIRACLE

❖

Julian had always just accepted Bruce's presence in our house. They got along fine, for the most part, but Bruce played little to no role in disciplining my child. They were like brothers, I suppose, in a way. As Julian aged, Bruce started to go to PTA meetings and school conferences, but their talks about such things were casual and chummy, unlike my long discussions with Julian about his failure to meet with his math tutor or his constant disdain for gym class and gym teachers. I felt so hypocritical. I weighed at least two hundred and twenty pounds on a good, non-premenstrual day. I was unable to walk around the block without huffing and puffing. Reprimanding him about missing or doing poorly in gym class made me feel like the biggest hypocrite ever. But nothing up to now had made me ever change my mind or see myself as a fat woman. I was fat and I knew it, but I was happy. I was insulated. Strange men wouldn't dare approach me sexually and I liked that. It removed me from critical social situations, and I was never, ever, ever promoted at work just because I was attractive. It was never an issue.

Julian had Victoria's Secret and Budweiser calendars in his room since he was thirteen, and I knew he was having wet dreams. I even heard him masturbating in the bathroom from time to time. However, with all my worldly knowledge, I wasn't prepared for the kind of porn I found in the bathroom, attached by a painstakingly clever little set of hooks that snagged around punched holes in the side of the magazines and a protective plastic sheath, fastened to the inside of the tank. I hadn't seen porn in over twenty-five years, not since the playground of my youth, when I was practically captain of the smut team. This was hardcore lesbian fetish stuff, stuff I was unfamiliar with and again, unprepared for. I had never seen a vagina that close before—not even in books. Nowhere.

I was curt to Julian all day and he finally asked me what was wrong. I just chickened out. When Bruce came home, I took up the issue with him.

"Did you look at porn magazines when you were young?"
"Yep."
"How old were you?"

"I guess about eight." He scratched his beard. "My grandfather got *Playboy* and he kept it under the bed."

"Really? Then this is normal?" I asked and showed him the copy of *Vicious Cherry* that I found. He turned bright pink and couldn't seem to keep from smiling.

"That's mine. I guess you found it in the toilet tank?" he asked.

"Oh," I said. "Oh, well then. Yes."

He laughed a little bit. "I read it for the articles."

"I can see that," I laughed.

We sat on the bed holding hands for a bit. I was staring at the floor at a tube sock that had its white fuzzy inside pulled through.

"Am I not attractive to you?" I asked.

"Kar, come on. It's not about that. It's just a magazine."

I was quiet. I was humiliated and I didn't know why. It was easy to see that I would not be as attractive as one of the supermodels or even someone older and fatter. It was easy to see why he should get off on women in leather. It was all so easy to see I didn't know why I never saw it before.

Christmas, Valentine's Day, my birthday, Halloween. So many reasons and occasions to buy chocolate and candy. I'd pass the Godiva store in the mall and I'd have to look. I'd purchase a pack of m&m's at the pharmacy, but I'd get the king size because it would be only twenty cents more. I remember when I was starving, when I would step into a restaurant, surreptitiously look at the clientele as if searching the faces for a friend's, take three or four starlight mints from the bowl near the register and step back out into the cold, only that and a chocolate chip cookie to live on for the next three days. But now I could afford any food I wanted. Now I'd buy a twenty-four candy pack from a gourmet store for twenty-four dollars. Quick, it's opened and I've eaten two, three, more. This is where I've learned to fail as a woman, as a person. This is the reason for my girth: I pay in pounds of flesh.

"I guess I don't have to talk to Julian, huh?"

"Karen, look at me." I looked. "It's not a sex thing. It's just a thing. I like to look. I still look, but I only touch you."

"I don't feel right after this," I said.

"Don't ask me to give this up. I don't think there's anything wrong with it, and I never have. And I won't start thinking that there's something wrong with me now. It's a guy thing. I'm sure of it. It's natural."

Part of me wanted to look at it, to share the "guy thing" with the guys, but the other part of me said, "not in my house."

"Do what you want," I said, and left.

I went to the grocery store. I walked around all the vegetables laid bare in the produce aisle and they all looked like perversions. I stared at soup labels, but I was preoccupied. Before I knew it, I was looking at the magazines. *Teen Beat, Tiger, Elle, Mademoiselle, Esquire.* They all were the same, hawking garbage. It made sense why he would look. Here was some skinny model wearing next to nothing, looking like a teenager. Here was some boy decked out in leather. It was all the same with a little less clothing, a little more titillating. Of course, I thought. It's about attitude. I can do that, I thought. And I did.

❖

For the next year, I ate less, cooked healthier, didn't eat after nine pm, gave up ice cream altogether (which was painful, awful, the hardest thing to do in the entire world), walked briskly and eventually started to jog. And as a matter of course, I lost weight.

I have to say that I've always had excellent resolve and the French bikini I bought that same day after shopping at the supermarket did it. I went to Macy's, bought a size eight bathing suit and brought it back to Bruce. I said, "If I lose enough weight that I can fit into this and be photographed, will you promise to not look at any more women?"

"Deal," he said.

So that's what I did. When I felt thin enough that I had to replace most of my clothes with size tens, I tried on the suit. It looked good. I had no idea how much I weighed (for some reason my scale got hooked at 175 and never reset to zero) but I decided I was ready. I called a photographer and made an appointment to do some sexy shots.

I chose a studio that said it did this kind of thing and the person who took my call was a woman. She told me she set up a session with Jan. Jan, to my dismay, was a guy. He had steel gray hair combed back in a plait. He had me lie down in the bathing suit against a silk cloth and he took about eight photos. I was heavily made up, and he asked me to wash off my face.

"You have no idea what I can do with an airbrush," he said.

I was aware of the feeling of my skin on the fabric and was awfully uncomfortable. I wondered what else he might airbrush.

"Do you use this silk sheet with everyone?"

"These kinds of photos, yes. But it's just been dry cleaned."

I stood up and felt my belly, thin with muscles but still a nice protective layer of flab over my gut.

"Okay," he said and rubbed his palms together, the rings on opposite hands making a *click*. "Now for the nudes."

I felt hot and tired. My back ached and I felt a little nauseous. I felt vulnerable. Of course, I was naked, but I felt naked because I was thin. He wasn't naked. I was naked. I was the one with the body in front of the camera. I had everything to fear.

"I'm done," I said.

"Just a few more, sweetie, and then you can get some dinner."

I was too hot and the floor seemed to be getting away from me. I lost my balance completely when I undid my bra.

"I'm done," I said and gathered my clothes, regaining strength.

"You're the boss," he smiled, obviously aggravated.

I ducked behind a screen that was set up, ludicrously, for changing. I dressed quickly and paid him in cash. I rehearsed what I would say to Bruce when I would tell him that I chickened out, and that he had won the right to look at naked women for the rest of his life.

I drove home in a panic and realized that I cut off two cars before I pulled to the side of the road and let myself breathe. To my surprise, I cried. I needed to cry and so I cried. I didn't cry because I failed, but because I was finally breakable. I had made myself able to be destroyed, easily destroyed. But before I was fat, and I was grotesque. I could never go back now, I thought. I was open and without a solution and I had done this all to myself. It was idiotic. I wiped my tears with a paper napkin from my purse. I was hungry again.

I navigated the Volvo to the 7-Eleven nearest our house and bought a big box of Twinkies. I asked the polite Indian woman behind the counter to hand me a couple of the porno magazines. She held up a copy of *Jugs* and smilingly asked, "This one all right?"

I agreed and took three others. I paid for it all with a twenty dollar bill, crisp and illicit, Andrew Jackson's bloated face chiding me silently. "Thank you! Come again!" called the little gray cashier as I heard the door bell chime on my exit.

When I got home, I wrapped the magazines in a big blue ribbon and presented them to Bruce ceremoniously. He cheered for me and for himself. We talked about the shoot as I curled onto the sofa and dug a spoon into the white flesh of a grapefruit, (I left the Twinkies on the passenger's side seat of my Volvo; the box stayed there for two days, the whole weekend, before I noticed I hadn't slipped from the diet) and I told him everything except about me crying. I left that for myself, private time, a knot that I would give myself the space to unravel as I needed to. We watched reruns of *M*A*S*H* and fell asleep together, the magazines still curled beneath his arm.

❖

The chicken pox struck both Julian and Bruce at the same time, when Julian was sixteen. Bruce was much harder hit and harder to deal with. I made repeated trips to the store for ice cream and calamine lotion and microwave popcorn and Neosporin and band-aids and root beer and out to the video store for awful Tony Danza or Judge Reinold movies. I could barely stand to be in the room with the two of them, Bruce stripped down to his boxers and a tee-shirt, much too small now because of a short cavalcade of medical scares due to the onset of chicken pox so late in life that landed him on steroids and bloated his idle body to nearly twice its original bulk in two weeks. His chest hair pressed against the white cotton and I watched his yellow fingernails loosening just scabbed over scars, creating red blooms in the threads of the cotton. Julian lay in plaid pajama bottoms, his bare thin chest sprouted only one or two migrant hairs that were thick, like insect hair. He was covered in red bumps that he dared not scratch for scarring, but he rubbed a vellux blanket over his back and arms. I was afraid that the vellux would pick up the infection and spread it to other parts of his body. As they watched *Going Ape* for the third time in two days, I busied myself loading the neglected dishes into the dishwasher and wiping down the kitchen counter that had puddles of old milk and coffee grains spread across it. Just as I sprayed the third coat of cleaner across the gray formica, the doorbell rang.

"Who is it?" Bruce asked me from the other room. Instead of bothering to answer him, I went to the door and looked out the pickled glass window. It was a man with a full beard, dressed all in black. He looked Hassidic, wearing a hat, but without the curls.

"I don't know," I answered as I swung open our front door. It actually took me a minute to place the face, just enough time to give him the opportunity to take advantage of the open door and step inside. He could see my guard was down. He looked beautifully familiar, like a family member, like someone I had once grown used to seeing every day of my life. And it hit me: the face was Julian's. Welcome home, Abraham.

I was so scared I felt my bowels sink. Flight or fight. I was a little mouse sweating and scurrying against the inside of a metal cage. My heart was beating so hard I thought my eardrums would burst. I held my breath, waiting for the panic to subside.

"Looks like you've done well for yourself, Karen," he said, peering into the living room. Julian was propped up on the couch to see who it was, but his naked foot dangled over the arm rest. I heard Bruce get up, and in his boxers, too-tight tee-shirt and little red blood stains, he was the most imposing, threatening man I'd ever seen in my life. However, graciously, he extended his hand to the stranger.

"Bruce," he said.

"Abraham. I'm the boy's father."

Bruce's hand dropped back to his side. He looked at me and I shrugged calmly. I felt somewhat nauseous, but I felt stronger having Bruce next to me. It occurred to me that this was a true thing between him and me: that I could rely on him in times of need, and I couldn't picture a time that could have occurred to me at which I might have needed him more. Julian scrambled up to meet his father, a man smaller and frailer than I remembered. It was as if the years had sucked height out of him. I saw through the window that there was a blond woman in the car, and the motor was still running.

"Do you want to invite her in?"

"Nah, she's..." he didn't finish. I could tell now, from the way he was glaring at Julian that he must have been tipsy if not drunk. Julian wrapped his blanket closer to his body.

"Chicken pox," said Julian.

"Oh. Oh, I see."

"I'll get you some water," I offered. "Or coffee. We can catch up."

"Jesus, Karen, he's beautiful. He's fucking beautiful. I got five kids now other than him and they're all little ratfaces compared to this guy. He's a fucking Adonis!"

"I got the coffee," said Bruce. "Set him down in the living room."

None of us moved, though. The light was off in the foyer and I was increasingly aware of the darkness, even though it was light enough to see everyone's features. I think I was aware that it would be bad for your eyes in this light if we were reading, though we weren't. I broke the circle that our bodies defined by stepping over to the switch. As soon as I turned on the light, I saw the woman in the car look to the house. Our eyes met for a moment and then she looked away to the dashboard, perhaps to change the radio station. She didn't seem to be the first wife that I remembered.

"Karen, you look good. I mean, you're, you were always a big woman."

"Thanks," I said. "You can get out of my house anytime you want."

"Ma," said Julian, "Is this him?"

"Yep." I wanted a cigarette. I really wanted to look a lot more casual than I felt.

"You're my father?" he asked, as if he couldn't get his mind around the small body in front of him.

"I'm your spitting image! I'm your father! Look at me. You got every single feature I have. We look exactly alike except for the pimples, but you'll grow out of that. And your height! You're a beauty, a fucking racehorse!"

Julian started to cry. Abraham lifted his arms to accept my bawling son, but dropped them.

"What is this? I come all this way to find my son and he cries. What is this?"

"Why are you here?" I asked.

"We were at a colleague's home for dinner and I had your address and..."

"How did you get the address?"

"We have ways..." he said and smiled, wagging his finger at me.

"How long have you known where we live?"

"For a while. For years."

Julian interrupted, "So why now? Why did you come here now?" Bruce returned empty handed, but I heard the coffee maker gurgling. He had also put on jeans and a sweater, both still awfully tight around his midsection. He put his arm around Julian, but Julian shrugged it off.

"It could have been any time. Is now a bad time? I said we were in the neighborhood. You don't know how many times I wanted to call," said Abraham. I listened to his voice, searching for what had made me love him so much. I wanted to hear it, like on an answering machine, over and over, to study it.

"But you never did," wailed Julian in a throaty adult pitch. I got the sense that this was his voice, that it was no longer going to grow any deeper than this weird wobbly wail. "I never knew I had a father. Mom told me that you wanted nothing to do with me and I accepted that. It was your bargain. You did this. You are not welcome."

I felt like a terrible mother. I should have done something earlier, driven by the asshole's house, pointed at him while he watered their rose garden, told him what a mistake it was to get involved with this snake. I should have prepared him for this moment, as inevitable as it was, but I don't think I wanted to believe that he would be able to find me. I think that's what it was, that I was selfish and thought that I was done with this man, that his commitment ended at my pregnancy and I could disappear with a child that looked just like him if I wanted to. But once Julian left my womb I forgot that he would grow up feeling like half a person, with a mysterious Y chromosome that somehow got stamped there. It wasn't enough. I needed to teach him how people you think are going to be there aren't going to be there when you really need them. And when you are finished needing them and you are able to roll on your own, they come back and attack you. All your defenses are gone. You never expected the thing you knew had to happen to actually happen. You got tired of waiting. You put down your gun.

All of my hatred was gone for this man, but Julian's was out of control. That half that was unfilled was obviously stuffed full like a locker with rancor and hatred and shame. I saw how hard it must have been for Julian all these years, accepting Bruce as an avuncular booby prize, going with the flow, wondering what was so wrong with him that his father would leave him *in utero*. No wonder why he had four mirrors in his bedroom; he had no idea who he was.

"You don't talk to me like that. I'm your father," said the funny looking little man standing in my foyer. "I love you, son."

This was a lie in a house in which I had disallowed lies more than ten years ago. Julian took a step in front of Bruce, stopping him, and slapped Abraham on the side of the face. Abraham gaped in horror as his cheek turned pink.

"You are nothing to me. Never come here again," said Julian. Again, I shrugged. I was completely satisfied, I had to say.

Bruce walked the confused Abraham out to the car. The pretty blond woman slid into the driver's seat. Unspeaking, she smiled and waved at the three of us as she drove away. I wondered if she spoke any English.

We went back to the couch, Julian and I nestled into each other, like survivors of a storm. Bruce stretched across the floor, looking at the ceiling. We put the Tony Danza movie on mute and listened as Bruce told dirty jokes, one after another, until we couldn't help but laugh.

9. What Else I Know About Love

My mother called to tell me that my grandmother was very sick. When we arrived, the table was arrayed with cold cuts, Kaiser rolls, wheat bread and condiments. There was a plate with pickles and one with cole slaw, pungent and vinegary. We had a choice of tomato juice, V8 or Clamato to drink. While Julian and Bruce wiped their red mustaches away with the backs of their hands, I opted for tap water.

"One glass of tomato juice is half of the vitamin C you need for a day. Did you know that?"

I smiled and drank my water.

"And there's no cholesterol."

Although I didn't grow up in this house, I still felt young and worn down again in my mother's constant presence. It's odd how even though she switched perfumes and the smell of the whole state is different, and even though she lives on the water, where the gulls swoop low overhead and the salt from the ocean wears down the pebbles that make up her yard and scrubs the paint from the dilapidated houses, she maintains that same farmy smell in her skin that she earned from all those years in Barnesville. We never had much of a farm, not more than a couple horses, some pigs and a chicken coop, but the dusty smell of infinite flat land that had been overgrazed by recent cattle and the smells of onion grass, sassafras and hemlock never left her nutty brown skin. She bustled like a woman who still had small children in tow, deftly stepping over the cat though she never looked down to note his position in the kitchen. The guys retired to the living room to watch sports (any sports) or midday HBO on her twenty-five inch bunny-eared television that was older than Julian and to chew on their second sandwiches. My mother started in.

"So, how much did you lose?" she asked. I could feel the fingers kneading into my skin, probing for a weakness. What had I done so wrong?

"Twenty-five pounds, maybe. Maybe fifty."

"Ah, you're a chemist and you can't count."

"Does it matter?"

"You look thin."

"I looked fat before."

"All I'm saying is there's a balance."

"And you're saying I missed it."

"You look tired. Have the V8—it has potassium."

"Ma…"

"I know, I'm telling the chemist what has potassium."

"Is it going to be like this the whole time I'm here?"

She balled up the hand towel in her hand. The duck print on the side was pulled taut within her fist and the breast of the fowl swelled out at me like a threat, its one eye wary. "Tell me something," she said.

"Shoot." I looked away from the duck and scraped at spilled drying mustard on the dull veneer of the kitchen table.

"Why is Bruce in my house? Do I tell people he is your fiancé? Do I tell people he is a man you live with? What?" She let go of the towel on the table. The swollen duck crumpled into layers of fabric.

"You know Bruce. You've known Bruce for years. You know he takes care of me."

"You are too old to not have a legal thing. What happens if you die? Do I get Julian? Can I be sure of that? Do I get Bruce too? What happens then?"

"Mom, Grandma's not even dead yet. Women in this family never die."

"I had a sister who died at nineteen."

"Did you?" This was new information.

"Yes, I did. There's a lot of things you don't know about me."

"I don't doubt that."

"When was the last time you went to see your grandmother, by the way?"

"I went a year ago, with Julian."

"She's very sick. She won't be with us much longer."

"She's one hundred and two. I hope she won't be with us much longer."

"Shut your mouth."

"I take it back, I take it back, I'm sorry." I didn't really mean it the way I said it. I knew it was a terrible thing to say. "I just meant that she's probably miserable."

"Yes, I pray for God to grant her a peaceful death during her sleep. I pray for that everyday. You should go with me tomorrow. And bring Bruce."

"You can tell her that he's my husband. We'll buy some thirty cent washers at the hardware store and pretend they're rings."

"She'll be mortified that she wasn't invited to the wedding. I'm sure she'd be happier if you were living in sin."

Bruce walked in with his empty glass of tomato juice. He nodded and said 'hey,' to my mother. He chose a roll, split it with his huge fingers and started to slather some mayonnaise on it before he noticed me glowering at him. "Maybe later," he said. "I really appreciated the first two sandwiches." Once my mother looked down, he pinched his face at me and I stuck my tongue out in response. When he got into the other room, below the clearer din of the war movie that was on, I heard Bruce and Julian chuckling, no doubt about me.

My mother sighed as she gathered up the plates with obvious clattering and placed them into the sink. I had to offer to do them, and she knew it. Of all the things we mutually lost, her power of guilt over me was still alive and kicking.

What Happened to the Miracle

❖

I wore a skirt to see my grandmother. I wore a skirt because my mother wouldn't take me if I wasn't dressed properly and jeans wasn't properly. The skirt was one of the very few items of clothes that remained in my mother's house when I moved away to college. My mismatched blouse was twenty years out of date. The only other option I had, which I pointed out to Julian, was the pant suit that he asked me to wear to the jamboree when he was four years old. He shrugged idly at me, and continued reading his Truman Capote book. I wore the red and brown plaid wool skirt and yellow blouse.

The last time we saw my grandmother, she was moving around the nursing home using a rolling walker introducing us to all of the other denizens of the nursing home. However, since her second stroke, she had lost all control of the left side of her mouth, so everyone's name was a permutation of three of the five or sometimes six vowels. She showed me her newspaper for the day and pointed to articles she wanted me to read. After a while, she snapped the paper out of my hand and forced it into Julian's. She clapped her hands together twice every time he read a paragraph.

Now she was flat, like a slip of paper in an open book of bleached white papers. There were three tubes going into her—one taped to her hand, one into her nose and one that snaked into the sheets and it remained a mystery what it carried in or out. I asked my mother what exactly was wrong with her. "She's old," she said, as if I were the kind of negligent daughter that she just knew she'd have. But I felt terrible when they began talking. My mother interpreted all the mealy vowels as if they were straightforward English. She told us that her friend Harold Buxton who was eighty-nine had just died last week. And then she said, "But I outlived him!" And then she told us that Gordon Conroy, who was seventy-three, had died. Again, she repeated that she had outlived him. She did this with a long series of contextless individuals known by their first and last names and ages at death, and each time, like a mantra, said that she had outlived them.

I saw what kind of world my mother had grown up in, to be raised in a house who was fiercely competitive even until now, on her deathbed, when she is barely holding on, her framed letter from Bill Clinton congratulating her on her one hundredth birthday on the wall behind her, pictures of her and my grandfather who was taken from her in D-Day, pictures of her and my mother, and a little blond child whom I suspected was a daughter, who may have similarly disappeared like Anna May did. It had been easy for me not to ask about that little fair haired girl in the pictures, to assume that she had died early, as a child, or to assume that she, too, was taken by the promise of greater things, California, fame, drugs, rebellion, whatever. I asked my mother then, "So what happened to your sister?"

Grandma's eyes grew wide and she let out a long, exhausting string of vowels and shook her finger at me. When she was done, she lay back on the bed, taking deep breaths, but keeping her one good dark blue eye on me, watching for any sudden moves. My mother held my grandmother's hand during this tirade and closed her own eyes, hushing her down. As my grandmother finished, my mother stroked her hand, shushing and calming her. She turned to me and said out of the corner of her mouth, "Later."

Later was not to come until after my grandmother died, three days later. It was a peaceful death, in her sleep, probably dreaming of all the other people in the world who died right before she did.

❖

Later meant that we would be poring through our family history for days, my mother talking freely about all the dirty skeletons she had kept locked up for decades. It meant that we would be closer than we'd ever been and I would understand more than I ever had. But I have to fill you in on the background first.

I loved Anna May, and love her still. I have said mostly the good things about her because I guess I still want to honor her. She could be a terrible person, though. She had awful fights with her girlfriends, and she lived dangerously with boys, so that they clamored for her attention. Nothing was good enough for her when it came to boys. Her jewelry box was stuffed with gifts that she never wore. Sometimes when we were going out to the movies, she would put some of the jewelry on me. Once she gave a guy a black eye because he saw us walk into a stationary store and he grabbed me asking where I got the necklace that he had given her. Boys wrote her poetry and letters and sent her flowers. It wasn't everyday that she would receive gifts, but she was so casual about them each time they arrived that it seemed more often than it actually was.

Her female relationships were extremely short lived. If she happened to have a girlfriend last for over a month, it was a success story, someone she could brag about as being her very best friend. It was easy for her to turn against girls because she always felt like she was in competition with them. If a female friend won the affections of a boy in school, regardless of whether he was popular or not, or interesting to her, she would go after him. Most times, she won him over, too. Unfortunately, she never found what she was looking for in them.

She preferred television to books and movies to television. She preferred dates and dinner and dances to them all. She loved moving around, being the center of attention, being hated and loved.

To her female and male friends, she always referred to a mythical "best friend in the whole world," named "Judy." "Judy" was the result of her conversations with me. Sometimes she and I would lie on the ground in the dusty earth behind the McMayer's wheat field and she would ask me how I felt about things, felt about the world, felt that very day, waking up.

"Isn't it just the most precarious thing in the world that we wound up to be human beings?"

"I guess," I'd say. "But it's pretty simple. We're people."

"But our spirits could be in absolutely any thing. Even if we are made up of a whole bunch of cells and bacteria and stuff, isn't it weird that we are still us?"

"I can't imagine being anyone else," I'd say.

"Me either. That's what I'm saying!"

I never corrected her assumptions about science. Maybe that's one of the reasons she loved me so much. But anyway, we would have these lovely deep conversations that really got to the heart of her philosophy of life, ill-formulated perhaps, but deeply running.

She would tell her friends at school or her boyfriends that she had had the conversation with 'Judy,' since it wasn't very cool to be quite so intimate with your baby sister.

One day, not long before she left, one of her boyfriends was clamoring to meet "Judy." He wanted them to double date with his friend from college. Oddly, Anna May, who was trying on the name "Cerise" at the time, agreed. She got me all dressed up in her sexy baby blue go-go boots and a white fringed dress (I was in the between stages of having a figure, but for some reason I believed her when she said I looked great. I still believe her. I believe that she believed it) and walked me downstairs to meet her boyfriend and his college friend. Buddy, a TKE from Ohio State, was not pleased with me, but I dutifully answered to the name Judy all night and gave my fifth-grade educated opinions on such topics as what age you should go all the way (according to my calculations, I had six more years. It took me almost eleven, though), what movie star had the most staying power in the limelight, and which got you drunk faster, vermouth or sloe. Buddy, whose Christian name was Philip, gave me a very generous good night kiss on the cheek when they dropped us off at eleven-thirty. As my mother screamed and ranted about us being out so late, I mooned over the wet medallion souvenir of my first date, my night with Buddy who was a college boy. She smeared cold cream across my face, trying to erase the orangy red smeary lipstick that Anna May had carefully applied before we left. I fell asleep dreaming of talking all night about those simple dilemmas people on dates have: hamburger or cheeseburger, Coke or Pepsi, third base or all the way. I'd have been willing to have modified my answer to any of them on his account.

"Judy" was not Anna May's only invention. She created circles of friends who would believe her when no one else would. If she said she was out with bikers, she usually was, but if she said she was out with a bunch of intellectuals, you could bet that she was out with the bikers or wandering alone along a lake nearby, practicing her speeches and what she was going to tell everyone when she got home. She was constantly escaping, calling herself a fair maiden or a roaring twenties high society debutante, or the most beautiful kind of person in the world: an actress. She even told us that she was Joan of Arc reincarnated once. I didn't believe her then, but I loved her. I never stopped loving her.

　　Anna May and my father never got along. For some reason, they were constantly fighting—physically fighting. I once saw her come up behind him on the stairs and push him. He caught onto the railing and swung around and slapped her in the face. If you were not Anna May nor my father, what you did when they were fighting was that you slipped out of the house as easily as possible if you could. Sometimes, you couldn't get there. One time I remember quite clearly was that I was cutting up a Holly Hobby book of paper dolls at the kitchen table and my father flew into the house raging about something he found in the barn. Anna May was thirteen at the time and she had taken a cigarette, God knows why, since she was so wild then, and put cigarette burns on the side of our horse, Lester Young. The little black burns were in the shape of a peace sign and each of them must have been no more pain than a bite of a horsefly, but it was cruel anyway, especially for someone preaching non-violence. He whipped off his belt and ran around the house. I could hear them rushing around upstairs, and stillness and then her stumbling down the steps in front of him, quicker and nimbler than he was even though she was encumbered by platform shoes. As per usual, I sat perfectly still. I put the scissors in my lap, knowing better than to brandish a weapon that might have been swept up by either party in the heat of the battle. I folded my hands. Every time they ran around the table, the paper dolls lifted and fluttered back to the table, and some slipped off to the side. I kept perfectly quiet, holding my breath, waiting for it to be over. She grabbed a fork from the silver case and he smashed a drinking glass. They ran around the table twice more, and incorporated me into a little bit of their drama when he lifted my chair with me in it and stomped it on the ground for emphasis. She stood directly opposite me, faking left and faking right. I kept my head down, watching her dark cherry reflection across the dining room table. Finally they were gone and I gathered up the paper casualties scattered across the floor, some large bonneted heads marked with shoe or stable boot treads or barn floor muck across them. Some heads were torn off completely. That's what you did in my house. After the cyclone of my father and my sister raged through, you assessed the damage and moved on with your day.

My mother and Anna May got along somewhat, but Anna May was just as much of a terror to her. Anna hung messages in her room that said, "Mothers are Weak," or "Think Global, Act Local. Kill Your Family." When I asked her about these things, she said they were only jokes and that you shouldn't ever hurt anything. I asked why she kept them up and she said, "To remind me that I get outrageously angry sometimes, so much that I can't control it, and that I need to find my center when that happens." She had several Transcendental Meditation books that she took out of the library which she never read. Of course, I read them. I would have liked to have helped her find her center, but it never seemed a good time once she'd lost it.

She went on hunger strikes and raged about my parents poisoning her. She got into fist fights with George. She and my father held their screaming matches, but she and I never had a disagreement in our lives. I was her respite, as far as I knew. I loved her desperately and always wanted to be like her. After she left, we left her half of our room exactly the same. I think we were all just waiting for her to give up and come back.

While she was gone, I went through all of her drawers. I put on her clothes and saw my rumpled eleven year old body failing to live up to the lush fabrics and demanding prints. I went through her diary, which was written in all block lettering. I couldn't bear to read it, though, after I saw how simple the sentences were. I entertained the notion for a while that she was a spy or an alien and that this diary was a simple decoy for one with absolute and integral information. My sister was always a simple girl. She had complex needs, but simple thoughts.

But mainly I went through her stuff because, of all the things that were bad that she did, what I think I despised the most was how invasive she was. She had no problem rifling through your coat pockets if she thought that you might have something she wanted.

She had no problem taking gifts from you if she felt she deserved them more or could put them to better use. She also had no problem looking through your drawers, under your bed, in your books, wherever she needed to. Unless you had something to take, she didn't take. Whether or not she ever used what she learned about you, I never knew. As I said, I was never on the receiving side of her wrath.

When it was clear, after about three years, that she wasn't coming back, my mother packed up all her things and moved them to the basement. They sat against an old black trunk that I had always assumed, correctly, was my grandfather's army trunk from the war. There was a big brass lock on it and I didn't ask any questions. Truthfully, I was afraid that it was his bones in there, or something hideous and scary. The truth of the trunk revealed itself with my mother in her living room.

When my mother moved to this house, the movers had stowed the trunk in a crawlspace in the attic. It was extremely difficult for my mother and me to maneuver the heavy item out of its space, but we managed it. When we opened it up, millions of questions about my heritage fluttered up at me and were answered all in the same gesture. I waited for my mother to begin.

What my mother told me was the story of her sister, Karen, born in 1931 to Grandma Isabelle, who just died. Not only was Karen born out of wedlock, but she was mildly retarded. It was not severe enough that she was a danger to herself, but it was bad enough that she would never complete eighth grade and would remain mentally a little girl until the day she died.

Isabelle, my grandmother, was the daughter of a stockbroker who had been doing famously on Wall Street and a mother who moved in the upper-class circles at the time, eating dinners at the Algonquin, but not at the round table. Isabelle married a soldier in the Army named George Henry Eden in 1923 but he was still stationed in Fort Benning while she stayed in New York City waiting for him she attending debutante balls of her unmarried friends until he came back an officer in 1927. They lived in the penthouse apartment with her mother and father for two years while the young couple looked for a house in Virginia so George could start his political career. When the stock market crashed years later, in 1929, her father killed her mother by pushing her out a window. He tossed the family dog, a spaniel named Gordon, out after her and then shot himself in one of the many suicides precipitated by the crash.

Isabelle and George were unable to claim anything on the life insurance policy that covered both her parents, and as most of her father's money had been moving in stocks and bonds day to day, they inherited next to nothing. They sold the penthouse and moved to the Bronx in a small Italian neighborhood. One night in July of 1931, while George was at an Army friend's funeral in Oklahoma, Isabelle was raped as she was carrying home groceries. The police report, which was kept and sealed in a cellophane bag, read in large, childish handwriting that she had been carrying "ice cream, vanilla, and Chesterfield cigarettes." It was a man named Sgt. Brimley that signed the police report. Also in the trunk was a telegram to George Henry that had informed him, briefly, that his wife was in the hospital and that she had "been violated." When he got back, he didn't find out much more from talking to her as she mentally blocked out the entire thing. Up to her death three days ago, she refused to admit it, even though the culprit was caught in a matter of days and put in jail and the result was her pregnancy with Karen.

George had a terrible time reconciling the fact that his wife was not capable of handling the truth about her child and that night. He desperately wanted to get out of the city; everyone who passed him was a possible suspect until the actual rapist was caught. Isabelle would not attend the trial, insisting that he had not violated her, but that "he had passed her in the night, not looking this way or that, just a simple fellow unconcerned with me, a blissful middle-aged matron." George watched the baby swell in her belly and it pained him terribly to imagine the kind of monster it might grow up into. He was glad when his wife gave birth to a girl. Isabelle took pictures of Karen Sophia and showed her off to all of her female friends, the debutante crowd, who knew about her misfortune but said nothing. They cooed to the baby, bouncing her on their laps and smiling at her with sympathetic eyes.

George moved Isabelle and baby Karen to Ohio where Isabelle was miserable and alone. When the war started, he reenlisted as an officer in 1939, leaving his wife with Karen and their four-year-old, Mary Leigh, my mother. George never returned from the D-Day invasion, and my grandmother was left with no one but her two daughters. No longer the New York starling debutante, but a gray-haired Ohio widow, she hardened. She found a job as a secretary making seven dollars a week. Because they were so poor, Karen was not able to get the educational and developmental attention she needed and my mother became her caretaker, even though she was two years younger. As soon as my mother was fourteen, she took a full time job in a soda shop and Karen was left home to her own devices during the day. Most of the time she read books or went to the movies or did chores without any problems.

My mother met my father at the soda shop, when he would come in and make polite conversation with her after eight every night. His father was a rancher who wasn't doing very well, but he said that he aimed to make the estate good when he took it over. They dated briefly and were married in 1950, because my mother was two months pregnant.

Unbeknownst to the newlyweds, Karen was also pregnant; it was assumed that, while she was hanging the laundry, some teenage neighborhood boys coerced Karen into having sex with them in a nearby abandoned tenement apartment. From what she reported to the doctors (details the boys themselves corroborated in court), she had been going with them after school at least three times a week for several months by the time she became pregnant. She died in childbirth at nineteen. My mother said that she and her mother knew what was happening to Karen only because when my father came over once, Karen climbed onto his lap and pulled up her shirt, exposing her breasts to him. He was so disgusted with the display that my mother made her weekly visits to her mother's house for half a year by herself.

Even though until her death my grandmother never ever admitted that she knew that she had been raped in the Bronx, when she called the police to report what had happened to her daughter, she asked for Police Sergeant Brimley and told the secretary to "let him know that it's happened again." There were no other flaws in her testimony and when she was asked to clarify who Brimley was, she refused to admit that she had ever requested him.

Karen died giving birth to Anna May, two weeks before George was born to my mother. In our house, growing up, they always celebrated their birthdays together. My parents were encouraged to tell people they were twins. Because I was so much younger, I was more a distant witness to their friendship and love and I guess I always did assume that they were twins. Anna May used to tell me that her birthday was not the same day as his but two weeks earlier. I knew from her Biology textbooks that it was physically impossible, but I was always willing to suspend my disbelief for her love. Now I knew that she was trying to tell me, in secret code, that she knew about her history. Seeing this trunk of artifacts all collected in one easy to get to place made it pretty obvious how she found out. It was clear why she left, now. She had thin ties at best to our family, a child borne from such miserable luck that she had to make her own history, find a story more beautiful, something to live up to. She went to Hollywood to find it. It's so poetic, really, that she should find her calling as an actress. She had unwittingly played a part for her whole life.

❖

Knowing all of this helped me only a little. It made sense to me now why she was treated by my family like she was, and why she was so close in age to my brother George. It helped me understand why she was much more beautiful than I was or my mother or any other woman on our side of the family ever turned out to be. What my mother may have intended was to distance her from me, to make me feel the rift of the family as a tangible space and to make me as disappointed in the situation as she had remained. I didn't. I felt the space all right. It was wide and palpable, but I still held a familiar hand. That hand kept its grasp over the chasm that my mother kept on trying to show me. I had a sister; for me, that fact still remained.

When my mother had cleaned out our house in Ohio, she gave me Anna May's clothes. They were the only hand-me-downs I would take, and some were so wild and eclectic that I never dreamed of wearing them. Anna May worked and worked to afford clothes that would live up to her and the speed at which she tried to live. She lavished these fabrics on me when I was small and she took hundreds of photos of me before she left. Los Angeles ate her and the photos were burned in a kitchen fire. I had nothing of Anna May but some old clothing and the sense that maybe I was beautiful once, in my loving sister's eyes.

I had these clothes in my closet in my bedroom. The closet space was meant for a family-sized mother and father, or maybe a yuppie couple with lots of coats, so there was plenty of room. These garments reminded me of her smile, her light, her energy. They explained to me what the differences were between her and me, our personal sibling rivalries, what she claimed dominion over, even in her absence, was fashion and beauty and joy. I got intelligence and honesty and laughter. We were still a team, best friends if I wanted to think of it that way.

My mother had her arms folded across her chest and one of her legs crossed the other. The top foot kicked out impatiently. "Well," she said. "What do you think of little Miss Anna May now?"

"I don't know," I said. "Do you want me to hate her?"

She uncrossed her legs and leaned forward. "I can't believe you. I raised her as my own daughter and you grew up knowing her as a sister and you think I want to make you hate her?" she paused. "I want you to forgive me and..."

I looked up, waiting for her to finish.

"Well, forgive me first," she said. "Then we'll discuss your obsession."

"My what?" I asked.

She looked at me out of the corner of her eye. "Do you forgive me for not telling you all this time? I couldn't because my mother hung on so long. I never knew that Grandma would be so old by the time we got to talking about this. She made me swear and I keep my promises."

"Yes. Yes, I don't mind that you never told me."

"I want you to see a therapist. I think you got an unhealthy obsession with Anna May. You keep her clothes and you keep her pictures. It's weird if you ask me."

"I didn't ask you." I heard Julian moving pots and pans around in the kitchen.

"Yes you did. But that doesn't matter. Are you going to go?"

"No. No. I think we're just fine here."

"You always know what's best. You always think you know what's best," she said. I was infuriated.

"I know what's best? You've been lying to me about my own sister for my entire life. I wouldn't be surprised if next year during someone else's death you pulled out a telegram and read it to me: 'Western Union circa nineteen sixty-nine. Found Anna May Edens Body stop Please Come Identify stop Repeat Your Child Is Dead stop Please Dont Alert Your Youngest Daughter stop Cause Her More Pain.'"

We were quiet for a minute. Then she said, "Stop."

"Mom, please tell me you never received a telegram, or a phone call, or anything and didn't tell me."

"I never did. Nothing. She was eaten up, just like we've all be saying. Disappeared. That is the truth about that."

I looked at the clock. It was three o'clock in the morning. My mother's face was drawn and exhausted, as if this secret that she had been holding all this time was a miracle to keep her young. It was gone now, released into the air, anybody's news.

"You're an obsessive woman. I've been reading about it. There's a woman I know who's like that and she just takes a pill and…"

"I'm going to bed. I'm really, really tired. I feel like sleeping for a million years."

A moment of quiet passed, perhaps the only real quiet moment my mother and I had shared when we were not trying to formulate our positions and argue the one another down. I remembered her dancing and singing in the kitchen the day I came home from college in 1979. Now we were truly quiet, truly tired. Her eyes closed and I was afraid she would ruin it by falling asleep. I put my hand on her arm, still crossed across her chest, protection from the chill of the old empty house, and I stood up. I kissed her forehead and she pushed her face forward to kiss my cheek. There was so much space now, so much of a large room in my soul, so few chairs taken up by a permanent audience. I cried for a bit out of exhaust, out of the truth, a bit for my grandmother because she had used her body and life as protection for her own brain, her own resistance to the truth. It was shameful, but poignant and human. It was something I never knew and only because it was hitting me now did I care. All of our women are such jelly on the inside, the Eden women, the ones who script such dark lies and then can't help but subscribe to them. My face in a jar by the door. Thank you, mother. I felt somewhat more free.

10. The Big Queen

Bruce told me a joke earlier this week. It goes like this: A gay guy decides he's going to come out to his parents. So he comes home and he decides he's going to tell his mother first, since she'll take it better. He tells her and she is silent for a moment.

Then she says, "So let me ask you: you've had oral sex?"

He says, "Yes."

"You've given blow jobs?"

"Um, yes...."

"So you've had someone's dick in your mouth?"

"Mom! Yes!" he says, exasperated with her candidness.

She straightens out her apron and says to him, "Well then, don't ever complain about my cooking again."

Kids were milling everywhere, boys dug through my pantry for peanut butter while girls were chopping up celery and apples; some kids had a few discreet six-packs on the side of the house and I saw no harm in that—it was the middle of the day. Kym and Chaney, two of Julian's best friends, were the darling hostesses of his graduation party. Their similar blond heads with jouncy curls bobbed around offering hors d'oeurves and soda, using my dinner plates as trays. Julian had finally made the honor roll and I saw no reason that we shouldn't celebrate, the kid and I, by surrounding him with people he loved. My mother was downstairs chatting and flirting with the teenage boys. They brought her lemonade, soda and a few mixed drinks. She was doing better than she could have done at happy hour. Some girls held their cigarettes awkwardly and many boys wiggled the necks of their ties. Bruce was tossing a football around with some boys in the yard. Most of these guys had stripped down to at least their T-shirts, and a few, their boxers. Bruce winked at me and blew me kisses between plays. I looked for Julian to give him his present.

There were gaps in the sects that I knew of, some kids had wandered out. In fact, it seemed that Julian had gone for a smoke with Darren. I couldn't blame them—I really wanted a smoke too. I knew I had a pack in one of the suitcases I haven't used for years. I pulled it down from the top shelf, but I heard something way at the back of the closet. Scared teenager breathing. I let it slip, "Oh, come on…"

I swept away the clothing that covered the perpetrators. I was more exhausted this time than curious, and I wished I hadn't looked. Both Julian and Darren were completely naked, and Julian was kneeling, one knee up, his terrified burning red face pressed against Darren's pelvis, partly blocked by Darren's wet, purple penis. Darren had his face turned away, wincing, pressing his forehead into the wall behind him.

My mouth was open, so I closed it. I looked down at my son, whose eyes were closed as if he were expecting to be hit.

I dropped my stare to the floor, knelt down a bit and said, "I love you," to my son. I whispered it. I wanted him to feel that, outside of this context, outside of this scene, his mother loved him, was not ashamed, was proud.

And I thought about the pink karate uniform and how he wore it religiously. My mind trailed across the obvious thinking that just because he wore pink, of course he was gay, but I couldn't believe that. Maybe it's just a different, freer culture now. Maybe he just doesn't know how to control himself; his hormones are raging so hard I can smell them. I thought about how I was always proud of him, for doing things that would make me wonder how his mind worked and what he wanted from life, and how much I love him for who he has turned out to be, how he grew into his own reactions to my teasing and egging him on. Maybe I am a terrible mother for this, but I love my son so dearly and I can say that now with no reservations. I never asked for him and I didn't ask for you to be here listening to me, but I know that I need you both so much to live and to be free...

My mother would have been horrified. I am free of her judgments. My mother would have cried. Or maybe she wouldn't have. Maybe we're just living in a different time now and what I accept from my son is different than what she accepted.

Of course I had left them then. I closed the closet doors and went into the bathroom. I looked at myself for a moment. I didn't know how to make this easier on these boys. *God, I hope Julian's in love with him*, I thought. *I don't want my son mistreated. I love him.* I reiterated. I hugged myself. *I love him.* But that meant something right there. He's going to leave me. He's going to fall in love and leave me, and that was something that I was not ever ready for. That's why I cried.

When I opened the bathroom door, Julian was lying against it, fetal, his fists covering his eyes. I bent down and put my head on his shoulder.

"You know I love you, honey," I said.

"I know."

I sighed.

"I'm not gay," he said.

"Okay."

"I like women too."

"Are you in love with Darren?"

He rolled back and looked up at me. "I don't know."

This was not the question for me to field. "I was in love with your father."

"Really?" He looked up. "You never told me that."

"I was. I am, I guess. I'm in love with the idea of him, how sweet he was to me and how much he wanted me. And I love Bruce too, but I don't know how to tell you how to feel."

"I feel, with Darren..." he began. "I feel, well...I want sex all the time. I want to touch him and I like when he grabs me, you know?"

"Okay," I said in my best encouraging upspeak.

"But maybe I just like to be grabbed. I kiss him. And he kisses me back. But when we talk, it's like, stupid. I don't know what to talk to him about. For a while it was just about wanting each other and how much we wanted to do it and then like, you know…" His eyes widened and he looked at me, willing me to understand.

"No. What?" More encouraging. I was really trying.

"You know. Butt sex."

"Oh! Okay?"

"But now we just do it, you know? It doesn't matter. I don't want to love him, you know. I want him to love me. Maybe it's just like and not love. I mean, I don't know if I want to be with a guy. Like, you can't marry a guy. It's not legal. And I'm not really totally gay because I'm really attracted to girls, too. Darren feels that way too, so I can't be totally wrong."

Okay. Here's where I stopped and realized that the heart-to-heart was really getting to be more of late night diner conversation. He was now propped up on one elbow and was talking openly, genially. I was still shaking, my eyes still quite blurred from rubbing the tears from my eyes. I didn't want to have this conversation like this. I think I even wanted a cigarette. Or a beer. Or something that could "go with" such a conversation. Something to casualize this. And the party downstairs, don't forget, raged on.

But we were so open with each other—we had fostered this relationship so he could tell me all of this and I would not be upset. The sides of my mouth twitched towards a terrific grin with celebration of this perfect frankness.

"Do people make fun of you or give you hell for being bisexual?"

"Oh, Ma! No way! No one knows 'cept me and Darren and Kym and Chaney. They're dating now."

"Really?" I had just caught Julian and Chaney kissing in our driveway not so long ago. It was strange to think of two high school cheerleaders as pretty and popular as they were trying out lesbianism. Julian was pulling on a string wearing away from the carpet. I tapped his hand.

"Where's Darren?"

"My room."

Sometimes in a wild range of emotions, your original emotion, the launchpad, I guess you could say, gets lost. I was upset but before I was upset, I was angry about two kids making out in my closet, against my clothes.

"Why," I swallowed, began again. "Why of all places did you choose my closet?"

"Do you really want to know?"

"Yes."

"Really? I mean, this is very very personal, and I might gross you out. It's a thing with me and Darren."

"Okay. I won't get grossed out."

"You know, it's something about the woman's clothes that you have in there. None of them are your clothes. I mean, I've never seen you in any of them, so they're not your clothes really. I don't know if you've noticed, but they still have the tags on them. A lot of them do. I think of it like a wasteland of woman's things, skins shed from centuries of fashion. I love the velvet blouses and the cotton. Darren loves to feel the linen. And there's a mohair coat that we rub ourselves against."

"You do what?"

Of course they were not my clothes, but Anna May's. The violation of these clothes was not so personal as it was tragic and incestuous, like the violation of museum pieces that reflect the history of your people.

Julian grinned. "I told you it might freak you out. But the deal is that we just got into touching and feeling. Stimulate the senses. And that's how we wound up together—he'd talk to me and touch my flannel jacket or I would see his new moleskin pants. And I had to show him your closet. Don't worry, it's not about you."

"It is most certainly about me!"

"No! No. You don't get it. It's innocent and natural and good," he insisted.

I don't know what he was going for here. I couldn't figure out his motivations for telling me this strange perversion as if it were just another lifestyle choice. I'm supposed to accept that my son likes to rub up against his mother's unworn clothes with his friends?

This is valid? "You've got to be kidding me."

"Look. Darren and I talked about anal sex, and you're okay with that, but you're not okay with something that he and I decided made sense: appreciating different kinds of material. Sensually. He read about touch in the Kama Sutra. You…"

"However, dear son of mine, there are many things in the Kama Sutra that you should not be investigating as a seventeen-year-old boy."

"I can't believe you. You don't know shit about intimacy."

"Go to your room!" I was on fire.

He smiled. "Good. Darren's on my bed…" He raced out the door to my room and slammed his across the hall.

❖

I guess I assumed that moving us from a city to suburbia would normalize us. I didn't think that anyone would notice me, being a single mother with a weird interpretation of how to raise my child. I think that I spent so much energy policing our relationship, scared that I wasn't enough for him, that I ignored the giant lack of our personal history. My own body, my own language, swelled to fill in those blanks. For that reason, I was to blame. I've never owned a camera, I throw away old letters. I remembered Abraham as tall, taller than six feet, and when he arrived at our door, I'm sure his size was more of a shock to Julian than anything else about him. I remember the farm in Barnesville as endless. Endless with boundaries. I gave my child a skewed history, not the truth, after I swore that I was doing right. So he made it up. He made up his own moral gauges and clues and sex with boys and rubbing against clothing and drugs all moved the meter needles within the white. What was in the red? I asked myself. I was terrified to imagine.

I descended the stairs. Dusk had settled in somewhat, but no one had turned on the lights. The faces were dark and obscured and the lesbian hostesses had given up on serving other people and were feeding each other ice cream out of the same bowl. I turned the light switch on and momentarily reduced the party to silence in the wake of the flood of light. I heard several high pitched voices exhale "Omigod!" and then the noise resumed to its old level. Bruce was running around in a circle outside, his arms above his head yelling out some long vowel. Half the kids playing were jumping up and down as the other half kicked on the dirt. The cigarette tips were little red insects now and I didn't smell only cigarette smoke.

I was so tired. My eyes were red and dry from crying and the air in my lungs felt too new as it does after a long cry. My legs ached, too, but I don't know why. I wanted to give Julian his gift, which was a computer. Instead of bothering with anybody, I sunk into the sofa in the den and put my head on the couch. And fell asleep.

Bruce woke me gently. I looked around to see black night out the window and then Julian holding a wrapped gift.

"Is it over?"

"Yeah." said Julian. He knelt down before me. "Most people went home. Darren is sleeping over but he's going to sleep in the basement, okay?"

"Um, okay." I was really tired. I stretched back and gathered myself back in. "Did you eat dinner?"

"Sure!" Bruce said. "Those kids ate nineteen pizzas!"

"Whoa!"

"We were hungry." Julian said. "We'd worked up an appetite." I flashed him an unappreciative look.

"I got your gift; it's in the garage. It's in a box." I wasn't making much sense yet.

"Whatever. We got one for you, mom." Julian handed me a small box. "Promise me you'll wear it."

"Okay." I said. I'd promised him slacks when he was four years old. Why not now?

I unwrapped the ribbon and tore off the paper. It was a long thick velvet lined box. Some of the afternoon was coming back to me now. God. I snapped the box open. It was a shiny diamond tiara.

"Cubic zirconia," Bruce said apologetically.

"Why did you tell her?" Julian whined. "It's the principle. It's the symbol of the thing."

I took it out and placed it on my head. "How do I look?" I could see from the shadows I cast that my hair was stuck up against my head from how I'd slept on the couch.

"You look beautiful, Mom."

"You look beautiful, Kar."

They stood regarding me long enough for my mother to round the corner, look at me and say, "Oh Good God!" and turn back the way she came.

This was my day, though. My son, my lover. My house. My life. This was the perfect day. We went outside to the balmy spring evening. Bruce drove us to the Stop & Shop and we each picked out a pint of ice cream. Bruce put his convertible's top down and we used little plastic spoons. I sat in the back. At a stoplight, a red minivan pulled alongside us, and the little kids in the back, a boy and a girl, stared at us. I didn't bother to wipe my mouth of its chocolate ring before I announced to their partly open window, "I'm the Big Queen for the Day! I'm the Queen!"

❖

My sister has never come back. I can only assume that she is dead, and in assuming that, I can only hope that she had a peaceful death with very little pain. Abraham did come back, again. Once. Julian was gone to college and Bruce was working. Abraham was not drunk this time and he told me about the blond, how they met, where his first skinny wife was. I remember asking him if he ever loved me. He said yes and took a drink of his ginger ale. His Julian's eyes danced above the tinkle of the cubes in the glass and I was so stricken that I looked away. He gave me a light kiss on the forehead before he left. I have my family now.

When he said that, I thought, you don't know what love is, but I think maybe he does. I think that maybe that's why he's been married so many times and so many times it's failed.

"It's work," I said, and he said "yes, it is. And I hate work."

We laughed some more and I told him some of Bruce's famous jokes. When I closed the door, I looked around my house. I looked in the mirror and saw Anna May. I was wearing her, my figure shrunk to her size, my face and cheekbones the same to a tee. She was in my mirror, for just a moment before I came back to me and she was right. She told me that I would see her again and I would know her. Her lesson was that people do change. They become different people time and again, and you can't look at someone for who you knew them to be. That's what age is about. If I had never chosen a Volvo, I think I might still weigh more than two hundred pounds. Or maybe if I'd gone with her instead of giving her to the police, I might be dead or starving or famous.

    I looked at myself and was glad, for the first time in my life, for real, that I was not a cricket or a spider or a bird. That's what she gave me after all.